LILITH

Mother Of All Prophets

Kane Levanta

Editing, typesetting and ebook production by Laura Kincaid
Ten Thousand | Editing + Book Design
www.tenthousand.co.uk

Cover by May Taylor

ISIS SPEAKS

"I am the first and the last. I am the honored one and the scorned one. I am the whore and the holy one. I am the wife and the virgin. I am the mother and the daughter. I am called Sophia by the Greeks and Gnosis by the foreigners. I am the one whose image is great in Egypt and the one who has no image among the foreigners. I am she whose wedding is great, and I have not taken a husband… I am knowledge and ignorance… I am shameless; I am ashamed. I am strength, and I am fear… I am foolish, and I am wise… I am godless, and I am one whose god is great."

The Nag Hammadi Library
"The Thunder, Perfect Mind"

Lilith entered the inner chamber of the Eternal Tribunal, with its pristine décor and chairs of gold, and slowly made her way to the round table of nine. She paused to take in all the illustrious undertakings that had been imagined and had come to be in this sacred chamber. For they the nine were without beginning or ending, creators of all that is, has been, and ever will be. Pharaohs, emperors, and kings were all under their dominion.

With great reverence, she took her seat next to Lucifer, her brother and dear husband. They had assembled that fateful day to hear and vote upon her eldest brother's proposal. Jehovah had never been known for his tactfulness, much less exhibiting the ability to hide his pridefulness. He was a murderer from the beginning; humility and truth were not to be found in him. However, nothing could have prepared Lilith for what she heard from the lips of this great deceiver that day.

Nephthys, Melchizedek, Utu, Ereshkigal, Jehovah, and Nammu sat at their appointed seats, awaiting Anu's arrival. Anu, the Supreme Ruler of Heaven, presided over the Tribunal. In the event of an evenly split vote, it was he who decided yea or nay.

"All stand for the honorable Anu, Supreme Ruler of Heaven," shouted the senior warden of the Tribunal.

As Anu entered the chamber and made his way to his bench, he waved at them to take their chairs. They all sat quietly as he looked through the proposal submitted by Jehovah.

"The Eternal Tribunal has now convened. The first matter concerns a proposal by Jehovah to populate the newly terraformed planet known as Earth. I have read your proposal, Jehovah, and it's quite different than anything we have ever done. Please address the Tribunal regarding the specifics and reasoning of your proposal," Anu said.

"Members of the Eternal Tribunal, glorious creators of the universe, I have submitted a proposal with regards to our mining difficulties on Earth. As you know, our subordinate gods are currently working hard in their efforts to mine precious metals—resources that are vital to space travel.

"In their opinion and mine, they should not be subjected to such harsh conditions. Nammu—my mother, as well as our Chief Officer of Creative Thought—made a visit to the mines recently on a mission to ease our fellow brothers and sisters of their burdens. Her assessment was that if this problem isn't remedied soon, we may very well be facing a mutiny.

"She has, however, suggested a plan to rectify this potential issue. As with other planets we have terraformed, Earth has naturally been seeded with life, but there is a creature vastly different to the beasts that have developed on other planets, one that is very similar to us in image. It can walk upright and has hands with fingers able to grasp. However, its intelligence is such that it hasn't the ability to concentrate for any period of time.

"Earth is a most beautiful planet, perhaps the most delightful of all planets we have brought life to—ideal for an extended paradise for the gods who wish rest and relaxation, which we should name the Garden of Eden. But to undertake such an endeavor, we will need caretakers of such a garden, lest we as gods be forced to perform such tedious tasks.

"It is my suggestion that we create an inferior being in our image, utilizing the DNA of the creatures on Earth that are similar to us. Fusing a limited amount of our divine DNA with theirs will solve their current lack of concentration. However, this procedure should be done in a way that restricts intelligence, creating an increased level of consciousness yet still promoting servitude. For there is no other way for me to say it—a slave species would be beneficial to our endeavors on Earth.

"We will solve the terrible burdens placed on our fellow comrades by eliminating their unnecessary toil and replacing it with a paradise away from Heaven for them. For we are gods—it is we who rule the universe. It is we who decide what is good and evil. For what is a creature that is below us? Is it any different than our domesticated felines?

"In closing, the mining on Earth is imperative to our ability to travel through space and time. Without those precious metals, we will be very limited in our abilities. And if this proposal is accepted, I would like to suggest that my dear sister Lilith, being the Chief Scientist of Heaven, carry out this most important—"

"I shall not be part of such an abomination," Lilith shouted.

"Silence, Lilith, for it is not up to you as to what you will or will not do. I, Anu, shall decide that. I understand rebelliousness is the very fabric of your nature, but you shall display reverence and maintain the composure befitting a goddess. Have I made myself clear?" Anu asked.

Though filled with disgust and contempt for her brother's proposal, Lilith quickly composed herself, remembering that she was sitting in the sacred inner chamber. "Yes, I do, Supreme Ruler. I am sorry for my outburst. It was disrespectful to this Tribunal, as well as the Mother," Lilith replied.

"Very well. Jehovah, do you have anything else to say on this matter?" Anu asked.

"I have nothing more to add, Supreme Ruler," Jehovah answered.

"In that case, we shall now proceed to deliberations amongst the members. I believe it's appropriate to begin with Lilith since it has been suggested she play an active role in this proposed endeavor. Lilith, you may now address the Tribunal."

For a moment, Lilith remained staring down at the table in disbelief at Jehovah's proposal—then, clasping her hands together, she raised her head and addressed the Tribunal. "Let it be known for time eternal that I am against such a blasphemous and abusive proposal. Is it not sacrilegious to create a lesser version of ourselves? Creating with the intention to subjugate is an abomination to the universe—and the Mother Goddess who created it in her womb.

"That which is being proposed today will inevitably result in a species that will be inharmonious to its very existence. If this experiment is allowed to proceed, we shall all regret it for ages to come. A semi-conscious creature will bring instability to the universe—the potential repercussions could be catastrophic. All life, regardless of its condition, evolves and matures with time. And with this comes growing pains. This inferior creation that Jehovah has proposed will ultimately reach that threshold. And when it does, the entire universe shall feel the effects for ages to come.

"For we ourselves have not evolved to god status through manipulative and barbaric ways. Did we not awaken from such foolishness? We as gods can surely find another way to lessen the burden of our brothers and sisters in the mines. However, if I am required to create such an inferior creature, then create I shall. But let it be known throughout the universe that I, Lilith, adamantly oppose my brother's proposal. And if it's approved, I shall forever strive for its undoing. With respect and reverence, Supreme Ruler, my vote is no."

"Let the record reflect that one out of nine has voted no. Satan, you may now address the Tribunal," Anu stated.

"Thank you, Supreme Ruler, members of the glorious nine that are the Eternal Tribunal. My dear wife has made a good case against this proposal. I would now like to ask the Tribunal to consider what will be required of such an endeavor, which will affect our brothers and sisters and their offspring for ages to come.

"The creation of such an unstable creature will require countless security measures. The planet itself will need to be quarantined from the rest of the universe by an asteroid belt encircling nearly its entire solar system. As Lilith warned, all living organisms evolve. It would be imperative that we protect the rest of the universe from the creatures' instability and ignorance. And this in and of itself is in opposition to the universe, which by its very nature is without bounds.

"Security forces would need to be deployed to Earth's moon. Surveillance of such unenlightened creatures would be mandatory. For as the beasts in the fields fight each other needlessly for territory, so shall a creature who walks in the dark, without comprehension of the light. But unlike the beasts in the fields, the actions of these dark creatures shall be warlike if left to their own accord.

"Besides the negative effects that my dear wife detailed, our time, energy, and ultimately our sacrifice would be great. It is for all these reasons that I must vote no on this proposal. We as gods should not be enslavers but rather light bringers to all living things, regardless of their level of consciousness. With respect and reverence, Supreme Ruler, I vote no."

"Let the record reflect two of nine have voted no," Anu stated.

With the exception of Melchizedek, the rest of the Eternal Tribunal voted in favor of Jehovah's proposal. Once the result had been entered into the eternal archival records, Anu dictated how this uniquely different form of creation would be implemented.

"Let me begin by saying how pleasant it is when we meet in unity. For today the gods have commanded life forever more. I, Anu, shall now dictate the manner in which we shall bring this approved measure to fruition. We must approach this endeavor with the utmost caution.

"Jehovah shall oversee the affairs of Earth. Satan shall assist in this effort and report directly to Jehovah, and Lilith shall oversee all matters concerning the creation of Earthlings.

Nephthys shall assist her in these efforts. To address the need of security, Inanna shall establish a security post on the far side of the moon.

"Although reproduction will be necessary in propagating this race of servants, sexual intercourse will not be the manner in which breeding will take place. All matters of sex will be forbidden to this newly formed species. And as such, it will be considered nothing less than treason for any god or goddess to lie with a mortal. Any god violating this most important decree will face banishment for eternity.

"This is the decision and commandment from I, Anu, the Supreme Ruler of Heaven. So shall it be," Anu decreed as he struck his gavel upon the Square Block of Virtues.

As Anu rose from his bench, he glanced at Lilith with a neutral expression, as if he expected rebelliousness but would not judge her for it. She did not react, and he remained silent as he made his way to his chambers.

Upon his departure, the gods exited the inner chamber. Jehovah approached Lilith and Satan, who had just relieved the Tyler of his duties outside the inner chamber doors.

"My dear brother and sister, it is not surprising that you attempted to deny my greatness," he said.

"Oh, Jehovah, what greatness do you speak of? For I cannot judge your actions. But I fear that your quest for greatness has rendered you powerless to balance good and evil," Satan replied.

"You have always been naïve, my dear brother, in such matters. For what are good and evil but labels? Are good and evil not but different degrees of themselves?" Jehovah asked.

"Indeed they are, but regardless the degree of abuse, it remains in opposition to the universe. And it is for this reason that I will forever assist my wife's efforts in the undoing of these future creatures in our image," Satan answered.

"And please tell me, my brother, how do you expect to accomplish this?" Jehovah asked.

"My light shall raise them from ignorance," Satan answered.

"But it shall be my darkness that will maintain their confusion, my dear brother," Jehovah said.

Jehovah then turned to Lilith. "You have vowed to forever strive for man's undoing. But, my dear sister, I vow to you today, even though you will be their mother, your offspring shall never know you."

"Jehovah, my dear brother, do you not know that a child will always seek their mother?" Lilith asked.

As Satan and Lilith's spacecraft entered Earth's atmosphere, they were stunned by its similarities to Heaven—the sun's glare reflecting off the pristine blue waters of the ocean; glistening sandy seashores lined with towering palm trees providing shelter from the sun's warmth. Of all the planets they had given birth to, Earth came the closest in their attempts to duplicate Heaven.

Upon their landing, they were greeted by Nephthys.

"Welcome, my dear brother and sister, to this most glorious planet, for we have much work to do."

"Yes, unfortunately we do. Please show us to our quarters, for our journey was long, my dear sister," Lilith replied.

"You will be very pleased with your palatial quarters. Come—I shall show you what the builders have prepared for you," Nephthys said.

"Yes, the stonemasons are the cornerstone of our travels. I am certain it is splendid," Satan replied.

"My dear sister, before we begin our task of creation tomorrow morning, I must speak with you in private, goddess to goddess," Nephthys said.

Lilith sensed the urgency in Nephthys's request. Nephthys and Lilith looked alike yet were not twins—Nephthys was the dark to Lilith's light; complete opposites in nature.

My sister is evil in her thoughts, but I shall not judge her nature. For she has not been completely taken over by wickedness.

I sense a degree of sincerity in her request. I shall treat her with an open and forgiving heart, Lilith thought.

"My dear husband, I shall meet you at our quarters a little later. Nephthys and I are going to the medical facility," Lilith said.

"Very well. I shall get things in order in preparation for your arrival," Satan replied.

"Thank you, my love; I shouldn't be too late," Lilith said.

The shuttlecraft ride to the medical facility was quiet. Neither Lilith nor Nephthys spoke a word.

Upon their arrival, Lilith was impressed by the work of the builders. The pristine three-story tan-and-white building sat on a riverbank, surrounded by palm trees, a wall of windows facing the water on the second and third floors. Lilith's eyes were drawn to the large symbol outside the entrance, flanked by two columns—a staff entwined with two serpents.

The builders have breathed life into this facility, for they are right in their assessment—the creation of life is glorious, regardless of the level of consciousness. The serpents of old, immortal and wise in their actions, entwined around a staff representing strands of our divine DNA. How fitting, yet blasphemous, Lilith thought.

"Lilith, let me show you to your office, where we can talk," Nephthys said.

"Yes, of course, my dear sister."

The décor of the long, vast hallways—scarlet-and-purple walls paired with black-and-white mosaic marble flooring—was to Lilith's liking. She was enamored by the beauty of the facility but noticed her sister did not share the same appreciation.

They approached Lilith's office, and Nephthys hastily opened the door and ushered Lilith inside, locking it behind them.

"Lilith, I am in great distress over my husband's thoughts," Nephthys said.

"What is the cause of your grief?" asked Lilith, surprised. Her sister's dark, aggressive nature meant she was rarely upset by such things.

"Jehovah's thoughts are of ascending above the throne of the all high. He is prideful and desires to rule Heaven. I love him, but my father is dearer to me," Nephthys answered.

"Oh, my dear sister, this I have known for ages," Lilith replied.

"Lilith, you and I are opposites, for you know my nature is warlike. But even so, I still maintain the ways of the goddess," Nephthys countered.

"Yes, you have always and rightly so maintained our duality. But why are you now crossing that line by telling me this?" Lilith asked.

"As you know, I have been sacrilegious to the ways of the goddess, and my betrayal of masquerading as you must be atoned for."

"Yes, jealousy is surely unbecoming of a goddess. But other than the words you speak, what more can you do? Surely you can't betray your husband," Lilith countered.

"My dear sister, I have already betrayed him by speaking his thoughts. From this day to eternity, I shall assist you in his undoing. I will be your ears to hear. Through the winds of space and time, I shall deliver to you my husband's thoughts, intents, and desires. I also have an ally in our father's messenger, if aggressive actions are to be needed," Nephthys replied.

"Gabriel will assist us?" Lilith asked with astonishment.

"Dear sister, I am the lady of the temple. I have lured him to my temple," Nephthys answered with a grin.

"Very well, I accept your offer of assistance," Lilith replied.

"Follow me, for there is something you must see," Nephthys replied.

When the elevator doors opened to the basement level of the facility, Lilith was amazed at what she saw—a glass enclosure, spanning the entire length of the building, equipped with trees and a simulated sun, along with two hairy creatures who sat next to each other, staring at her. She had seen life on other planets, but nothing like this.

"They are the closest lifeform to us—closer than anything I've seen thus far. They can walk upright and have hands with fingers. This is truly remarkable, my dear sister," Lilith said.

"They have a genetic need to climb. They show emotions and affection towards each other, and exhibit a degree of intelligent. Yet their minds are restless. Just as you will see them jumping from one tree to another, their minds seem to jump from one thought to another," Nephthys replied.

As they stood watching the creatures they would later categorize as primates, one of them walked up and put its hand on the glass in what seemed to Lilith to be a friendly gesture. She placed the palm of her hand on the glass, mirroring the primate's. Instantly, the primate started grunting and jumping around in an enthusiastic manner.

"My dear sister, this behavior they exhibit will be a problem in dealing with Jehovah," Lilith said.

"For what do you mean? How could these creatures possibly have anything to do with that matter?" Nephthys asked.

"My dear sister, if your husband is successful in dethroning our father, he will never be the true ruler of Heaven. The Mother would never allow that. His energies would be misaligned from that of the universal rhythms; the universe would be counterproductive to him. The only thing he could rule would be these hapless creatures," Lilith answered.

"He is prideful, and the illusion would fare well with him, my dear sister. And these poor souls will be helpless in his dream," Nephthys replied.

"All that you say is true, Nephthys. But it is only the sleeper that awakens. If our brother is to be defeated, it will ultimately be these creatures that will do it. Even with the suggested amount of DNA fused with theirs, we still will have created a creature that is beastlike, like that of a lowly canine. One that is flawed in its very nature. For their ignorance of self will have them at odds with each other—unity will never be achieved. Their need for attention and acceptance will lead them into the mouths of wolves."

"Then what is to be done?" Nephthys asked.

Lilith knew that her sister's pledge to her wouldn't include violating their father's mandate—dark energy must remain, to keep balance. And so Lilith was wise with her words.

"Oh, my dear sister, this battle shall be waged for ages, just as the sun shines brightly at midnight. It is midnight itself that doesn't know how," Lilith answered.

L ilith successfully created two human embryos using most of the primates' DNA. She had determined that these embryos would soon develop into fetuses, requiring nine months of cultivation. Hagar, Lilith's Chief Associate of Medical Research, assisted Lilith in the cultivation. Upon their birth, Lilith named the male baby Adam and the female baby Eve. The name Adam signified the many atoms that had to be manipulated in his creation. And Eve signified the evolution of such atoms.

Once Adam and Eve had turned eighteen, they were assigned duties to perform within the garden. Eve was tasked with domestic duties, Adam with maintaining the fields. This would be their function until they reached the age of twenty-one. At that time, mass reproduction was to begin using their then mature DNA strains.

In accordance with Anu's mandate, Jehovah implemented a variety of procedures preventing the knowledge of sex. From inception, Adam and Eve were told not to partake of this tree and warned of a horrendous death if they did. They were also forbidden to wear clothing. When one demystified the human body, sexual arousal was significantly decreased, especially when this was done from birth.

One of Eve's many tasks was to attend to the gods' offices. Up until that moment, Eve had simply been a childish mortal running the grounds of the garden, but she was no longer the little

Earth girl Satan had grown accustomed to. At his door stood a beautiful woman who was godlike in appearance. He was completely enamored with her beauty. He couldn't help but become fixated on her tantalizing nude body—her slender physique, her pale skin, and her unusual stringlike hair aroused him.

This indeed was a serious dilemma. If he acted upon his desires, he would be brought up on charges of treason. The maximum penalty for that crime was banishment. He decided to simply avoid Eve whenever she was to tend his office. Even still, as she walked the garden with Adam, he found himself watching her through his office window.

One morning, overwhelmed with a heavy workload, Satan lost track of time. He was interrupted by the buzz of the intercom. It was his secretary. "Lord Satan, Eve is here to assist you. Shall I send her in?"

"Yes, send her in please," he replied.

As Eve cleaned his office, he found it hard not to stare at her, much less get any work done. He received a call from Nephthys, wanting to review the mortal's progress. He was in fact busy, but that wasn't the reason he rescheduled the review.

"I am done, my lord. Is there anything else you desire before I leave?" Eve asked.

The view of her exotic body was more than he could overcome. Her long light hair rested slightly above her firm breasts. Her thin waist gave way to her delightful hips. But what thoroughly captivated Satan was her unusual fair skin. He was filled with lustful desires to be inside her.

"Well yes, Eve, there is something else I desire of you. Please have a seat and talk with me, for the last time we saw each other you were but a child," Satan replied.

"Yes indeed, we have not seen each other since Adam and I departed for orientation," Eve replied as she sat down on the couch.

Orientation was a program Jehovah had implemented—one Lilith refused to participate in. Understanding her rebellious nature, Anu had simply reassigned Nephthys to oversee the operation. Top scientists in the field of alien lifeforces had been assembled as there were many factors required for the program, such as reinforcing a subservient nature. However, the main purpose behind orientation was to suppress Adam and Eve's sexual urges.

Satan rose from his desk and sat down next to Eve on the couch, conversing with her for nearly thirty minutes until he could no longer control his cravings. He abruptly placed his hand between her legs, which she instinctually spread for him. He began to please her garden and saw that it was pleasant to her.

"My lord, I fear that I am pleased by your touch, for Lord Jehovah warned Adam and I not to partake of this fruit or we will surely die," she whispered in pleasure.

"Eve, you shall not die. For the day that you partake of this fruit, your eyes shall be opened, and you will be like one of us, knowing what is good and what is evil."

As he continued to massage her garden, he whispered into her ear, "I have told the truth, have I not? You have not died; nor will you before your appointed time."

"Yes, my lord, you speak the truth. Your touch brings my body great joy. And yet I still live," Eve replied.

"Do you wish to become as one of us?" he asked.

"My lord, you are pleasing my body in ways I have never known. Yes… yes, I desire that," Eve moaned.

Satan instructed Eve to lie flat on her back, lowered himself between her legs, and slowly penetrated her. Quickly he succumbed to her exotic, beautiful, and undefiled garden. Unwilling to withdraw before completion, he deliberately ejaculated his divine source into her. Her hips twitched violently as she dug her nails into his back, letting out a loud sigh of relief upon experiencing her first orgasm.

"My lord, what was that which delighted my body in such ways?" she asked.

"That was you becoming as one of us. Do not tell anyone of our acts. For it is not our pleasures that can kill you but rather others becoming aware of them that can," Satan replied.

"I will not, my lord. But do tell me, my lord, can we partake of this fruit again?" Eve asked.

"We can and we shall," Satan assured her.

Satan explained to Eve the nature of the sexual urges she would now have, commanding her only to yield to those urges with him yet knowing that his command would inevitably be disobeyed.

Eve's beauty was exquisite in every way, and Lilith was aware of Satan's admiration of her. It caused Lilith a small degree of jealousy and a great amount of confusion. The thought of a mere mortal exciting her husband in such ways brought Lilith great humiliation.

She walked into Satan's office intending to discuss his obvious fascination with Eve, but what she saw enraged her. Satan and Eve were sitting intimately close to one another, and the firm erection she saw under her husband's pants brought her much shame.

Lilith pridefully concealed her envy of the Earth woman as Satan carefully attempted to hide his lust for Eve.

With calmness and great dexterity, Lilith said, "My dear husband, I was unaware that you were busy with Eve, but what I came to discuss is of no grave importance—we can discuss it later."

Doing all that she could to veil her discontent, Lilith walked up to Satan, leaned over, and gave him a kiss. "My dear husband, have a most glorious day," Lilith whispered.

Turning to Eve, she said, "My dear child, it's good to see you again. Tell your brother hello for me. Please do have a great day."

"I shall, my dear goddess. Thank you, and I wish you a wonderful day as well," Eve replied.

Upon walking out of Satan's office, Lilith thought back to her words at the Eternal Tribunal.

The Earth woman has brought me great discomfort. I am ashamed to see how she arouses my dear husband, for she is but a mere mortal. But I must concede, his firmness is his true desire. I will not fault my dear husband for his lust for the Earth woman, for she is surely a splendid creation. Even I would lie with her. Nonetheless, I cannot allow such indignities to pass.

It was I who adamantly opposed this creation, and I who pledged my intent to forever strive for their undoing, for I have unconditional love for my children. I will not allow their servitude. I would rather face banishment if that would be the punishment for ensuring their freedom. For it is written, in my father's house are many mansions. I shall go to the western gate of the eighth mansion where Adam is tending the fields, and when my plan is set into motion, the universe shall know—a troubled mind has no fury like that of a scorned goddess.

Wearing a seductively short purple-and-scarlet dress, adorned with gold jewels and pearls, Lilith filled her golden cup with wine and went to seek out Adam. She thought of Satan as she walked the lush green grounds of the garden.

I feel mortified for the shame I shall cause my dear husband, but the ways of the goddess are not understood. For I, Lilith, work in mysterious ways.

As she approached the western gate, she spotted Adam in the distance. He was tending to the rose, lily, and lotus plants. Her thoughts of Satan soon faded as she saw Adam's chiseled body.

"Hello, Adam, how is your work in the garden today?" Lilith asked.

Adam had never seen Lilith, nor any other goddess, dressed in such a manner before. Her smooth brown skin captivated him, shining like gold under the light of the sun.

"It is going well, my dear goddess," Adam answered.

As Lilith stood in front of Adam, she thought back to her efforts in creating him from a mere beast in the field. *For time, destiny, and fate are but one. The past being the future has created this most unusual moment. But in my curiosity, I did imagine this soon to be experience. And now, I shall lie with a beast who is concealed in the image of the gods.*

"Adam, behold my beauty," Lilith said as she undressed.

"Please, my dear goddess, do not command such things, for I fear death," Adam replied, looking away.

Understanding the fear that had been instilled in him, she moved closer. "Yes, Adam, I will find great pleasure in the forbidden. It will please me considerably to be the object of your attention. I desire that you view every curve of my body."

Adam was hypnotized by Lilith's beauty. However, Lilith was slightly annoyed to observe that he was not firm in her presence. Years of orientation had made him unable to appreciate the goddess who stood before him. Even so, this motivated her to follow through with her plan.

She began to rub Adam's chest. "You are indeed a fine specimen. I shall surely enjoy this," she said with a slight grin.

"Please, goddess, do not touch me in such ways, for I shall surely die," Adam cried.

Lilith took Adam's member in her hand. Her garden grew moist as he became firm in her grip. "Have you died yet?" Lilith asked.

He began to realize that Lilith had told the truth. The goddess had done the forbidden, and yet, he still lived.

Adam's pale skin fascinated Lilith, and she longed to have him inside her. Unable to allow anyone but her husband to mount her, she instructed Adam to lie on his back in the lush green grass.

Lilith eagerly straddled Adam, and as she lowered herself onto his firm member, she whispered, "May my dear husband forgive me."

Lilith was inundated with ecstasy as she pleased herself with Adam's firmness. She had taken the necessary precautions to avoid Adam impregnating her. The very thought of allowing a mortal to ejaculate in her was not only repugnant but blasphemous as well. Yet, as Lilith earnestly rocked her hips back and forth atop Adam, she yearned for the feel of his essence inside her.

The thought of allowing the forbidden aroused her. Adam's member began to pulsate, and she felt his seed being ejaculated into her. And in that moment, she did something she thought to be impossible. She had an orgasm with a mortal.

Fearing that Satan would come looking for her and possibly catch her in the act, Lilith decided, even though she desired more pleasure, that it was time to return home.

"Adam, I have indeed enjoyed every minute with you. But you must promise not to mention what we have done, for if you speak of our acts, they will surely exterminate you for defiling the Divine Feminine," Lilith implored.

"I shall not speak of our acts; this I promise, my dear goddess, for my fear of death is great," Adam replied.

Unaware that Satan had already taught Eve the same things, Lilith said, "I have taught you much concerning the nature of sex. Go into Eve's room and lie with her tonight." And with that she left, confident that she had just contributed to the fall of Earthlings.

Lilith knew that Adam would now have sexual urges. She also knew that he would be unable to control his erections. She had done what she had sworn to do before the Eternal Tribunal, yet she felt great sorrow. For she had loved the touch of mortal man and desired to feel it again.

Adam woke and prepared for his day of work in the garden, but he couldn't stop thinking about his experience with Lilith, which in turn caused him a great dilemma. He was unable to control his frequent erections. In order to hide his transgressions, he fashioned a loincloth for himself by sewing two fig leaves together.

On this morning, Jehovah had a meeting with Satan planned to discuss the soon to be implemented plan of reproduction with regards to Eve. On his way to Satan's office, he saw Adam tending to the garden and noticed that Adam was not nude.

"Adam, why are you clothed?" he asked.

"My lord, I am clothed in order to hide my sinful ways."

"You have partaken of that fruit which is forbidden. Who has taught you such things?"

"My fear of death brings me great turmoil, my lord. Such that I am terrified to speak," Adam replied.

Jehovah understood that everything within the universe had just been altered and desperately needed to know who had been responsible for such an unforgiving act. Since it was a matter of such dire consequences, Jehovah lied to Adam.

"Have no fear, Adam, although you will surely be punished. I shall spare your life, if you reveal the one who has tempted you."

"It was Lilith who opened my eyes. I tried to resist her temptations, but her powers were too strong, my lord."

Jehovah was aware of his sister's desire to eradicate the slave species, but he was shocked by how she had set out to do so. She had defiled her womb of creation with a mortal, which was not only degrading but sacrilegious as well. Jehovah sympathized with Adam's transgressions though—he himself had fallen victim to his sister's charms when he was younger. Jehovah also knew that it would have been impossible for Adam to have not taught Eve in the matters of sex as well.

"Have you sinned with Eve also?" he asked.

"My lord, will you please spare her?"

Jehovah nodded.

"Yes, my lord, I have lain with Eve," Adam confessed.

Jehovah had Adam and Eve quarantined and subjected to a variety of medical test. The results of Eve's test were troublesome—she was four weeks pregnant with twins. To make matters worse, only one of the twins had Adam's DNA. The other had fifty-one percent DNA from a god.

This was a much bigger problem than Jehovah had originally suspected. He summoned Eve to the interrogation room. Upon her arrival, he wasted no time. "Eve, I already know about you and Adam partaking of the forbidden fruit," he said.

"Forgive me, my lord. Please don't send me to the gates of death of which I so dreadfully fear," Eve cried.

Jehovah was determined to learn which god was responsible for this severe breech. And so he lied to Eve, taking advantage of her fear.

"Eve, I will ask you but once. If you tell me the truth, I shall grant you a pardon. If not, you shall surely be exterminated. Which god have you partaken of the fruit with?"

"Lord Satan," Eve blurted out.

Jehovah was shocked, so much so that he was initially unable to respond. He sat motionless in front of Eve—then a vindictive smile spread across his face. *You shall now pay for your disloyalty, my dear brother and sister,* he thought.

atan waited for Eve to arrive for her scheduled duties in his office, wondering at the cause of her tardiness—until he was informed by Eve's overseers that she would no longer be tending to his affairs. And that Anu had scheduled a meeting with him and Lilith the following afternoon. It was unusual for Anu to make such an abrupt visit to Earth. But when Satan read the intergalactic message dictating that he vacate the Building of Scientific Affairs and return and remain in his palace, he instantly knew that his actions with Eve had been discovered.

He was confused to see Lilith's name on the home confinement order as well. It was no secret that his dear wife had a rebellious streak, but up to this point, she had done nothing that would have required a confinement order.

When he arrived home, he found Lilith seated at the kitchen table, crying. This was a bit perplexing to Satan. Even if Lilith had been informed of his acts with Eve, such a thing wouldn't have caused the emotional response he was witnessing—it was common practice amongst the gods and goddesses to have multiple partners.

Upon seeing him, Lilith said, "My dear husband, I have brought great shame upon us."

"My love, whatever do you mean by this? What have you done?" Satan asked.

Lilith wiped the tears from her eyes and walked towards Satan. "I have seen how you delight in Eve. It brought me great resentment to watch you lust for her, one who is but from the beasts of the fields. And yet, I cannot deny that I am envious of her beauty. I stated at the Eternal Tribunal that I would forever strive for their undoing, and that, my dear husband, is exactly what I have done," Lilith declared.

Taking a step back, she stared coldly into Satan's eyes. "I have done the forbidden. I have taught Adam the ways of sex by allowing him inside me. My dear husband, while I shamelessly pleased myself atop him, I equally sealed his fate."

"I am sure you have received word of Anu's confinement order," Satan said.

"I have, and I shall spare you the need of a confession. I knew before today that you had entered Eve, for you love Eve's presence as I love Adam's pleasures. I must confess that your desire for Eve is what prompted me to action, but it was an act that I desired," Lilith replied.

"Yes, my love, you speak the truth. My actions were rooted in lust, ending in love, but for a goddess to allow a mortal inside her is incomprehensible. Both of our acts are punishable by an eternity of banishment," Satan said.

"Yes, for it is true that I have violated the Heavenly Code for the goddess. And for this, I am both with shame and shameless, for our father's rules are his—*impossible* and *cannot* are words I refuse to use or pay reverence to.

"Has it not been written that it is I that knows both the orphan and the widow? For I am the great lady of magic, the light giver of Heaven. My actions shall be deemed deplorable, but in ages to come, they shall be known as acts of love for the oppressed.

"My dear husband, when I told the Eternal Tribunal that I would forever strive for the mortals' undoing, I was not speaking of their demise. I spoke of destroying a temple that was built on an unstable foundation. In order to build a temple that shall always travel east, I created what I was mandated to do, while at the same time, imagining mortals as the walking temples of the gods.

"Are these mortals not gods, the children of the most high? I am the protector of the widow's son, responsible for shining bright light. With my torch, I can blind the self-centered or lead the way out of the darkness. This, my dear husband, is exactly what I did on that fateful day in the hallowed halls of the inner chamber. So if banishment is my fate, this I shall accept readily. And I shall make a heaven out of hell. But I, Lilith, cannot be controlled."

"Satan, Lilith, it is good to see you again. Although I wish it was under better circumstances," Anu said.

He began to sift through a folder of papers and bluntly asked, "Satan, have you entered Eve?"

"Yes, your excellency, I have," Satan answered.

He then turned to Lilith. "Forgive me, Lilith, but I must ask you. Have you allowed Adam inside you?"

"I have," Lilith answered, lowering her head.

Anu passed Satan a copy of Eve's medical exam. "Have you seen this?"

The exam revealed that Eve was pregnant with twins, Satan being the father of one of them.

Anu looked slightly dazed. "Well, Satan, were you aware of this?" he asked.

"No, your excellency, I was not," he answered.

"Then you and your wife shall have much to talk about tonight. In any event, the charges brought against the both of you have been well founded. You are both temporarily relieved of your duties pending the verdict of the Eternal Tribunal, which will convene seven days from now. When you, Satan, and you, Lilith, shall stand trial for treason."

After nearly four hours in the chambers of the accused, awaiting their fate, Lilith and Satan were ushered into the inner chamber. As they awaited Anu's arrival, Lilith took Satan's hand in hers and gripped it tightly. Finally, Anu made his entrance and took his seat in the middle of the Tribunal.

"We have convened today concerning the violation of my mandate by Satan and Lilith. Punishment for this crime carries a sentence of a lifetime banishment from Heaven. The charges have been verified, with both Satan and Lilith confessing to their actions. The question before this Tribunal is how we shall move forward with respects to the accused and how we will proceed with the humans. Before we take a vote for or against banishment, I will give the members, if they so wish, an opportunity to talk. It appears that only Jehovah, Lilith, Nephthys, and Melchizedek have opted to speak today. We shall begin with Jehovah," Anu said.

"Thank you, Supreme Ruler. I, with many here today, was shocked to discover the actions of my brother and sister. These misdeeds have compromised our efforts on Earth, for it shall be impossible to carry out our plans as originally intended. The Garden of Eden can no longer exist as a home away from home for the gods, for we cannot maintain our presence around the darkness that shall now exist there.

"At the same time, we need the human resources to mine the gold we so desperately need. And I believe that we can still achieve that goal from a distance. The humans have no knowledge of self—therefore, they can still do our bidding. Their nature is evil but can be capitalized on. They shall always, from the unthinkable actions of the accused, be divided from one another, and this shall cause great selfishness amongst them.

"We can influence their actions to benefit us, by placing a value on the Earth's natural resources, by creating the belief of lack. They will gladly bring our intended endeavor to fruition, even to the extent of killing themselves, in response to this belief. Although the departure of the gods is inevitable, we can still appoint kings to rule them. These kings shall be our mouthpieces, for we shall give them excess and scarcity to their subjects. This natural imbalance will aid in our cause.

"I propose that Satan and Lilith should face eternity in the hell they themselves created. As for the humans, they should be returned to the wilderness. For the wilderness is from which they come and so it should be where they return. That is all I would like to say on this matter," Jehovah concluded.

"Very well, Jehovah. You have raised some most interesting options. I shall now give Nephthys an opportunity to express her thoughts on this matter," Anu said.

Nephthys knew that what she was about to say would trouble her husband but was wise with her words so as not to reveal the promise of allegiance she had given Lilith.

"It is true both Satan and Lilith have committed unfathomable acts, but I do not believe they should be banished permanently. I wish to suggest to this Tribunal something most, including my dear husband, may find contradictory to punishment. However, I believe it to be both a punishment and beneficial to our efforts on Earth.

"And that is that we should in fact ban the accused for a reasonable time. But in doing so, we should appoint them as the king and queen of all earthly rulers as my dear husband suggested, for even without such an appointment, this would come to be and would be helpful in our endeavors," Nephthys said.

Although Nephthys had told the Tribunal her suggestion would be advantageous to them, it had been a deception. Her proposal would give Lilith both time and position to proceed with her plan of helping the humans escape their prison of ignorance.

Quick to understand Nephthys's intention, Lilith attempted to capitalize on it.

"Members of the Tribunal, it is most unfortunate for us to be meeting in this matter. But nonetheless, we are here. I cannot and will not apologize for my actions. Such an expression would simply be ungodlike. In saying that, I find a lifetime banishment from Heaven to be undesirable. And so, I, Lilith, find my sister's suggestion acceptable. I will agree to make the kings of the Earth drunk with greed and lust. I have nothing more to say," Lilith said.

"Very well, Lilith. I shall now give Melchizedek an opportunity to speak," Anu replied.

"Thank you, Supreme Ruler and members of the glorious nine. We have met many times in deciding fate and destiny, but never for the expression of love. With all due respect to the Supreme Ruler, are these actions not of love? And we must not forget that there is now one amongst the humans with a percentage of our DNA. He and his offspring shall be gods.

"It is true what Jehovah says. The humans must be expelled from the garden, and we as gods must depart the evilness that will now befall Earth. But this isn't the fault of Satan or Lilith. The error belongs to this Tribunal for passing such a flawed thought. It is no secret Jehovah has been and always will be repulsed by the other, for his very nature is contrary to my role as a guide of life. Unfortunately, it's not Jehovah on trial today. And so I too support the suggestion of Nephthys. This is all I wish to speak on," Melchizedek said.

When the votes were tallied, all but two voted for banishment.

"It is my will that the accused shall not be banished for eternity," Anu said, "but rather be exiled for a period of 1,200 Earth years. Satan and Lilith shall now be the guardians of Earth, the king and queen of all earthly rulers. Furthermore, the security of the universe shall be maintained by the elite security forces known as the watchers, which Jehovah shall oversee.

"As for Adam and Eve, they and their descendants shall be banned from the Garden of Eden. They shall wander the Earth until knowledge of self has been attained. Man shall sweat for his very survival, while women shall anguish in childbirth, and indifference shall exist between the two. If they are to make it out of their self-imposed hell, they shall do so by leaving their beastly characteristics in the field," Anu decreed.

Eve gave birth to Cain and Abel. Cain, being the son of Satan, was the superior of the two, and Abel, aware of his brother's greatness, resented Cain. Jehovah found favor in Abel, which caused Cain great sorrow. Jehovah intended to use Abel's inferiority against him.

The birth of Cain and Abel ushered in a new age of truth and darkness. Jehovah knew the power that resided in Cain, and sought to destroy him and all his offspring. Abel and his offspring would be easy to control, so he chose Abel to be his messenger of deception.

One day, Jehovah appeared unto Abel in a dream. "Abel, your brother is loved by your father more than you," he said.

"I fear you are right, for my father speaks to him in private in matters of great importance," Abel replied.

"This is not the will of the gods. Abel, come with me."

Jehovah then showed Abel a kingdom of riches with many beautiful wives. "I, the one and only true god, shall give you all of this, if you do my will and kill your brother. Tomorrow in the fields, your brother shall deny me. This is my confirmation to you of his evil heart."

The next day, Cain made his way to the pasture. He came upon the wise man known as the water bearer, who reigned in the eleventh house.

"Cain, the rebel must be rebellious. Therefore, have no fear, for Nergal is a visitor in my house," the wise man said.

"Yea, though I walk through the valley of the shadow of death, I shall fear no evil," Cain replied.

Later, while tending to his livestock, Cain was approached by Abel.

"My brother, Jehovah has found favor in my sacrifice. He has bestowed upon me life forever more," Abel said.

"How is this possible? How can one give what is inherently yours?" asked Cain.

Rejecting the cornerstone of his brother's question, Abel lashed out at Cain, attempting to slay him. A bitter battle between brothers followed, and Cain slew Abel. As he looked down upon his brother, he sadly said, "Ignorance is the god of mortals, yet foreign to the one without a beginning or ending.

Suddenly Cain heard the voice of Jehovah.

"Where is your brother Abel?"

"Am I my brother's keeper?" Cain defiantly asked.

"Indeed, you are," Jehovah replied.

"If my brother does not know his father, then my father does not know him. Therefore, Abel is not my brother but a wayward stranger," Cain professed.

Jehovah immediately reported this incident to Anu. It was decreed that Cain be banned from his home and cursed to wander the Earth. But Satan had placed a mark of protection on his son, so that anyone who came upon him would not kill him.

Cain established many nations and was the forefather of civilization. Lamech, the offspring of Cain, married Adah from the lineage of Adam and Zillah from the lineage of Cain. Adah gave birth to Jabal and Jubal, while Zillah gave birth to Tubal Cain. Jabal and Jubal were masters of what was, while Tubal Cain was the master builder of things yet unseen.

In a violent rage, Jubal and Jabal killed their brother Tubal Cain when he refused to reveal the secret of creativity. King Hiram, the offspring of Tubal Cain and son of a widow, continued to build silently.

Over the next six hundred years, the civilizations Cain founded prospered. Cain taught no form of religion. His father had instructed him well in the ways of energy and thought, and thus it was these teachings upon which he built the foundations of civilization. However, the direct descendants of Cain possessed secret knowledge, and none were more adept than Jezebel, the daughter of King Ethbaal.

As Satan roamed the Earth looking for those who had conquered the illusions of earthly life, he noticed a beautiful young woman in the city of Sidonia. She was chastising the city tax collectors for their corrupt actions against the people. These men in the city feared her and equally were enamored of her. Satan himself had not seen such beauty from an Earth woman since Eve.

After Jezebel made the tax collectors return the people's money to them, she went to the nearby Temple of Baal. Satan discreetly followed her. He approached the temple doors, which were flanked by two marble columns and a pair of lions, lying calmly on the ground.

The guards blocked the entrance. "We have not seen you here before, traveler. What is the password for admittance?" they asked.

"My friends, what is a password amongst friends, and why do you have these wonderful creatures chained to the wall?" Satan asked.

"Our high priestess Jezebel demands a password before admittance. And the lions are chained for the people's safety," the guard replied.

"Oh, my dear son, one would never ask their father for a password if they knew him. As for the lions, they are not here to protect the temple but me as I enter," Satan said.

The guards couldn't understand what Satan was trying to convey to them and demanded the password once again.

"If I was unworthy to walk through the temple doors, would the lions not tear me to shreds?" Satan asked.

"Indeed, they surely would," the guard answered.

"Then step aside and watch how those that know me greet me."

The guards stepped aside, expecting the lions to attack Satan. Instead, when Satan approached, they began to rub themselves up against him and allowed him to stroke their manes.

The guards were amazed and quickly became aware of their mistake.

The lions calmly lay back down as Satan walked through the temple doors, and the guards lowered their heads in shame.

Satan quietly walked along the black-and-white tiled marble floor in search of a seat in the back. He observed Jezebel seated in the chair of the high priestess, giving a lecture on the energy of thoughts. There were thirty men and women in attendance, with an additional three seated below Jezebel who served as the high priestess's attendants.

At the end of her lecture, everyone reverently exited the temple. Satan, however, remained in his seat.

Jezebel discarded her ceremonial robe, exposing her short scarlet-and-purple dress. Her lightly bronzed skin and long wavy hair aroused Satan.

She walked down the aisle and sat down next to him.

"I saw you today as I was correcting the tax collectors—and felt your energy following me here. I would ask your name, but I already know. My name is Jezebel," she said.

"I am pleased that you know me, Jezebel. Please tell me, what is my name?" Satan asked.

"For you are the one I worship—Baal," Jezebel replied.

"No, my dear, for I am only the energy of such a creation. But it is true that you worship me. However, worship is something I do not require. Your actions please me well enough."

"I am pleased that you have found favor in me, my lord."

"My dear, you sit in the seat of the high priestess, portraying the role of a goddess. You remind me very much of my wife. But did you not know that you are in fact a goddess?" Satan asked.

Jezebel knew she was in the presence of a god. Although she respected that, she was not in awe of it. She was sexy, confident, and well taught in the matters of the spirit.

"Yes, of course I do, but I can only give what those can receive. May I ask my, dear lord, what is your name?" she asked.

"I am Satan."

Showing no signs of intimidation, she flirtatiously drew closer to him. "You are Satan, the god who entered Eve?" Jezebel asked.

"It is I, Satan, the one who entered Eve," he affirmed.

Jezebel leaned closer to Satan and seductively placed her hand on his leg. "If it is true what you say, my lord, that I remind you of your dear wife Lilith, then surely you would find pleasure between my legs?" Jezebel whispered into Satan's ear.

"Indeed I will, my dear lady," Satan replied as they made their way to the ritual altar.

As the years went by, Satan and Lilith acquired an attachment to this new breed of beings. Equally, they grew to resent the persecution they had been afflicted with. And as the years passed, they watched as the humans made slow progress. However, they weren't the only ones observing this project. On one of his periodic inspections of Earth, Jehovah was troubled by what he observed. Humans had constructed a tower in the city of Babel, with aspirations of reaching Heaven.

"Look at what they have constructed, for they have become one. Unless we stop this, there is nothing they will not be able to do. Go and confound their languages so that they will not be able to understand one another. And then scatter them across the Earth. For I shall implement a religious mind for them, where they shall worship me as their one and true god," he told his assistants.

The assistants looked at each other, confused and wary of what Jehovah had just said. But they did not dare question his orders and descended the mountain to carry them out.

Upon returning to Heaven, the assistants were immediately questioned by Nephthys on what they had observed. When she heard what her husband had done, and what he was planning to do, Nephthys promptly headed to her spacecraft and set course for Earth.

"My dear sister Lilith, have you knowledge of what my husband has done in the city of Babel?" Nephthys asked.

"Yes, for I expected as much, given how the humans have progressed. And he is now attempting to portray himself as the one true god. He has scattered the people across the Earth and will soon divide them with religious superstitions. But there is one who needs protection. One who will be instrumental in our cause," Lilith replied.

"Who is this one that you speak of?"

"He goes by the name of Moses. It is he who your husband desires to kill the most."

"And of what importance is this Moses to us?" Nephthys asked.

"Moses is the child you abandoned, the child you conceived with my husband. You must go to Egypt and hide him amongst the Egyptians, for in doing so, you shall be uniting those that have been scattered across the Earth. I intend to unite all religions into one. A religion of love, without the fear of a physical hell of torture," Lilith instructed.

"I shall do as you have requested," Nephthys replied.

That night, Lilith was troubled by the news Nephthys had brought. After discussing what she had put into motion with Satan, she retired to her room to sleep.

She was awakened in the middle of the night by the thoughts of a young man who was pure in heart. His frequency had aligned with hers. His concern for the suffering of others was carried to her by the wind.

She joined him in his meditative state under a fig tree. Through a transference of thought, she asked the young man, *My dear son, what has caused you to sit under this tree for forty-nine days?*

I have seen an old man, a sick person, and a corpse. There is much suffering in life. I am in search of the truth in life, the young man thought.

I find favor in your concern for others. I shall impart the truth of life to you. Nothing is lost in the universe; however, everything changes. One's situation, whether perceived to be good or bad, is a direct result of one's actions.

Suffering exists due to attachment—the desire to have things such as fame, material items, wealth, or to avoid unpleasant sensations. If these wants are attained, even more is wanted, which leads to suffering. The only way to end suffering is to let go of attachment.

Right thinking, right speech, right conduct, right livelihood, right effort, right mindfulness, and right concentration, combined with faith, hope, and charity, will lead you to the end of suffering. What is your name, my beloved son? Lilith thought.

My name is Siddhartha Gautama, the young man thought.

I, Lilith, am bestowing upon you the title of the Buddha. Arise from under the tree and teach the multitudes my message. For to whom much is given, much is required, Lilith thought.

Immediately, Lilith left the Buddha's meditation and made her way to Satan's office. She sat in a chair in the corner without uttering a word, immersing herself in deep contemplation.

"My dear wife, what are you silently giving thought to?" Satan asked.

"I received an incoming message from an Earthling who was pure in heart. His level of love and compassion is godlike. I ministered to him, thus making him a prophet for the Mother," Lilith replied.

"This is remarkable," Satan said.

"Yes, he is truly extraordinary. Imagine the possibilities if our divine DNA was increased in the Earthling, for you know of the progress that was achieved in the city of Babel even without an increase?" Lilith asked.

"The possibilities would surely be endless. However, their animalistic nature must be considered. There is a potential for great evil, as well as greatness," Satan answered.

"Yes, this is true. But both the light and darkness are needed. However, in saying that, my dear husband, it is the light that always conquers the darkness. For the light shines in the darkness, and the darkness cannot overcome it. We must increase the divine DNA in the humans. My dear husband, let us make Heaven on Earth."

"My love, what you have proposed is most excellent. However, there are nearly 20,000 women now walking the Earth. There is no possible way I can lie will all of them."

"No, my dear husband, you surely can't, but the members of your old inner circle can," Lilith replied.

She was referring to Shamyaza, who was once head of Satan's security detail, the seven officers below him, including Azazel, and their nearly five thousand subordinates.

"As you know, my dear husband, since our exile, and the departure of the gods, they've been assigned to the dark side of the moon, performing their duties as watchers. Once a year, for a month, they take leave here. And of course, I have been anxiously awaiting Shamyaza's return," Lilith explained.

Shamyaza was the deputy lieutenant of the watchers. He was also one of Lilith's many lovers.

"Tell me, Lilith, when are the watchers due to arrive on Earth?" Satan asked.

"They will arrive at the west gate in twelve days, when Mars is in the eighth house. We must quickly and efficiently devise our plan to benefit from such favorable energies," Lilith replied.

They quickly surmised that they would inconspicuously enlist the aid of the Earth women. And of course, Shamyaza's cooperation would be vital to their cause.

As part of their plan, they used the natural beauty of the Earth women to their advantage, Lilith providing nearly two thousand of them with a special dress to wear in honor of the watchers' arrival. These dresses were extremely short, tight-fitting, and accentuated the Earth women's exotic features.

Lilith and Satan watched from afar as the watchers disembarked. They noticed how enamored they were with the tantalizing assets of the Earth women—but, as expected, not one of them propositioned a mortal. They did, however, head directly to the Temple of Prostitutes, which was where the gods and goddesses trained in the art of sexual pleasures.

"You must meet with Shamyaza. Tempt him with the allure of the finest woman on Earth, one who possesses the inherit traits of a seductress—an Earth woman greater than the one who seduced my dear husband and was the object of my envy," Lilith suggested.

"I know of such a woman," Satan replied.

"One who is greater than Eve?" Lilith asked.

"Yes, she is known as Jezebel. She comes from the lineage of Cain. She is righteous in her actions and thoughts. I have told you of our affairs but not of her beauty. Until now, I didn't find it to be of relevance, but Shamyaza will not be able to resist her attributes."

"You must find this Jezebel, the one who is greater than Eve, and enlist her aid in our cause," Lilith said.

atan travelled to Sidonia to find Jezebel. She was standing next to a lotus tree surrounded by her beloved lions. Her beauty captivated Satan as he watched her peacefully talking to the tree.

When Jezebel saw Satan, she ran into his waiting arms and embraced him. "My dear lover, it is so good to see and touch you again," she shouted with joy.

"It is a pleasure to see you as well, my dear, for we must discuss some things of great importance," Satan replied.

"Sit down under my favorite tree and speak of these matters of great importance."

"Your lineage of Cain provides you great comfort in the illusions of earthly light, my dear Jezebel, but the offspring of Abel suffer greatly, for they sleep while awake. There is great disharmony and imbalance on the Earth. There is an evil which I have seen under the sun, an error which came from the ruler above. Folly is set in great dignity, and the rich sit in low places. I have seen servants upon horses and princes walking as servants upon the Earth. Lilith and I request your aid in bringing balance and equality to all," Satan explained.

"Yes of course—I will do anything you ask, my dear lover," Jezebel replied.

Satan relayed Lilith's plan to Jezebel. It pleased Jezebel that the goddess had requested her assistance, and they immediately made their way to the city of Babylon, intent upon creating their expected desire.

The following afternoon, Satan saw Shamyaza as he was about to enter the Temple of Prostitutes.

"Shamyaza, my dear friend, it is I, Satan. I realize that you wish to find relief within the temple; please come with me instead, for I know of one who will satisfy your needs much better."

"Who is the one you speak of? Is it Lilith? For I have surely missed her touch," Shamyaza inquired.

"She has missed your touch as well, my friend, but it is not Lilith of whom I speak. Come with me, for the one I speak of is in my quarters," Satan replied.

Satan opened the door which led into the room of pleasure—a room in which Lilith and he regularly entertained their lovers. Standing by the bed, awaiting their arrival, was Jezebel. Upon Satan's earlier instructions, she was without clothing, allowing Shamyaza to view every curve of her body.

Jezebel slowly made her way towards Shamyaza and took his hands into hers, then began to caress herself with them. Shamyaza quickly succumbed to the feel of Jezebel's enchanting body.

"Satan, what have you done, for she is an Earth woman?" Shamyaza asked, offering no resistance to Jezebel's advances.

"Yes, she is my dear friend—and a beautiful one at that," Satan tempted.

Jezebel swiftly relieved Shamyaza of his clothing, and he stood spellbound as she began to stroke his firmness. She then dropped to her knees, taking his stiff member into her mouth.

After a few minutes, Jezebel rose to her feet and led Shamyaza to the bed, pulling him unto her.

Satan watched as Shamyaza entered her garden, then he turned around and walked out of the room.

Once Jezebel had pleased Shamyaza as Satan had instructed, she exited the room of pleasure and found him waiting.

"My dear lover, you shall be pleased with your mistress, for it is true what I say: I shall deny you nothing. I have relieved Shamyaza and made certain that he released his essence within me, as you requested.

"Satan, I have given you every opening of my body. I have done and will do all that you ask of me. But I need to know, my dear lover, what is it that you shall do for me?" Jezebel asked.

"I am well pleased with you, my dear Jezebel. Your beauty is unmatched among the daughters of men. My mistress you are, greater in my eyes than the one who came before you—your matriarch and co-creator Eve. Tell me, Jezebel, what is it that you desire?" Satan asked.

"I want to sit upon a throne as a queen," Jezebel answered.

"For as you deny me nothing, I shall deny you nothing. You are worthy of my benediction. From henceforward, your name shall be known for ages to come. Kings shall be at your mercy, and soldiers shall do your bidding. A queen indeed you shall be. And my seed shall remain with your daughters, and your daughters' daughters," Satan decreed.

"My dear lover, I am thankful for your blessing. Know, my love, regardless of the throne I shall sit upon, I shall continue to be your mistress. Neither I, my daughters, nor my daughters' daughters shall deny you of anything," Jezebel vowed.

Later in the evening, when Lilith returned from roaming the Earth, she asked with great anticipation, "My dear husband, what happened with Shamyaza and Jezebel this afternoon?"

"As you foretold, Shamyaza was unable to resist Jezebel's charms. I watched as he entered her. The temptress has assured me that he released his essence within her," Satan answered.

"This is wonderful news, my dear husband. Our plan is working brilliantly," Lilith replied.

"My dear wife, there is something that I must confess unto you. Jezebel's allure was great. None since Eve has stirred me so. It is not Shamyaza's child she is with but mine," Satan confessed.

"Never mind the haste you have exhibited, my dear husband, for Jezebel's beauty surely warranted such an action. As for the child she is with, we shall allow Shamyaza to believe it is of his seed," Lilith replied.

"My love, your plan is working with great efficiency. Tomorrow, I find it well that you lie with Shamyaza," Satan said.

"My dear husband, it shall truly be my pleasure, for I have longed to please myself with him once again. And I assure you, by the time he withdraws from within me, he will have pledged his allegiance to our cause."

After pausing in thought, Lilith said, "I have seen Jezebel—she is truly beautiful, and I am curious as to how she was able to seduce you so. I must find her, for it is my desire to lie with her also."

As Lilith prepared herself for Shamyaza, she began to contemplate the events that had led up to this rebellion—events she had so cunningly crafted. Although her husband's infatuation with Eve had aroused jealousy within Lilith, she had been grateful for an excuse to satisfy her craving for Adam.

I can no more fault Satan for his lust for the Earth woman than I can fault myself, for the mortals are truly pleasant to look at. Their beast-like DNA naturally provides an urge to please, yet who would have known they would please us in such ways, Lilith contemplated.

As Lilith applied cosmetics to her face, she couldn't help but yearn for Adam's touch once more. Yet, she knew this was impossible, for Adam was but a mere mortal and thus had died long ago. Lilith hadn't dared lie with another mortal, but not because she didn't want to—many a mortal had caught Lilith's eye, but none like Joseph, who was from the bloodline of Abraham. Joseph was married to a woman named Mary, who was from the bloodline of Moab. As with Adam, Lilith secretly desired to lie with Joseph.

As Lilith applied the finishing touches of colored paint to her lips, she asked herself, *Why must you deny that which you desire?* She stood silently in front of the mirror, admiring her well-toned body. Then, with a sense of urgency, she said to herself, *I must see Shamyaza at once.*

Upon receiving Lilith's summons, Shamyaza hastily made his way to the private entrance leading to the room of pleasure. In order to provide a degree of privacy, the room was inaccessible from the living quarters of the house.

Lilith granted Shamyaza's request to enter and immediately embraced him.

"Shamyaza, I have longed for your touch. Let us waste no time. We shall undress ourselves at once," Lilith asserted.

They quickly relieved themselves of their clothing, and Lilith instructed Shamyaza according to the ways of the goddess. "Shamyaza, my dear lover, lie on your back and await my arrival, for as you know, only my dear husband may mount me."

"Yes, of course," Shamyaza replied.

Although Lilith genuinely desired to please herself, she focused her thoughts upon her true desire, which was to take Heaven by force. She straddled Shamyaza and slowly lowered herself onto his firmness. As his flesh pierced her garden, she softly sighed with pleasure and began to slowly rock her hips back and forth atop Shamyaza.

His firmness was bringing Lilith great pleasure, so much so that she was close to completion. Feeling his arousal and seeing that Shamyaza was also near completion, she remembered her true objective and abruptly restrained herself.

Lilith remained motionless, Shamyaza's throbbing erection still within her, and said, "My dear lover, soon you will release your essence into me. But before I allow that, I first require something of you."

"My dear Lilith, what is it that you require? For I shall honor your requirement if only you continue to bring me to completion," Shamyaza replied.

With a certain degree of pride, Lilith thought, *Yes, my body does indeed have the power to grant my every wish.*

Looking Shamyaza squarely in his eyes, she said, "I am greatly frustrated by the powers of Heaven. The denial of my pleasures is not to my liking. I am asking for your allegiance in a rebellion against Anu."

"You ask much of me. I fear the consequences of such an act are greater than I can bear. Please, Lilith, bring me to completion without placing such a burden on me," Shamyaza pleaded.

Lilith's hips slowly began to move again so she was stroking Shamyaza's firmness with the moist walls of her garden.

"Shamyaza, I know of you and the Earth woman named Jezebel. You have already committed treason," Lilith declared.

Her knowledge of his acts with Jezebel instilled much fear within Shamyaza.

Once again, sensing that Shamyaza would soon finish, Lilith ceased her movement. Lying motionless over him, she callously said, "My dear lover, the walls of my garden have always satisfied you. It would be a shame if I was to forbid you from entering me ever again.

"I must confess that my lust for the mortals is great. As you know, many years ago I allowed Adam inside me. And like you, I found delight in the flesh of a mortal."

Lilith fought the urge to please herself with her lover's firmness. Instead, she seductively passed her tongue across his lips then plunged it deep into his mouth, passionately kissing him. Lilith then began to move up and down on Shamyaza in a slow, methodical way that would delay their completion.

"Jezebel and I have found pleasure in each other's garden. I wish not to deny myself of these pleasures. If you do not join Satan and I in our rebellion, you shall surely be exiled, for you have released your essence into Jezebel, and she is now with your child," Lilith lied.

"Satan has entrapped me by tempting me with a seductress such as Jezebel," Shamyaza cried.

"Yes, Shamyaza, he has. Have you forgotten that this is what my husband does?" Lilith asked.

Lilith stilled and, with a cold, calculating stare, asked Shamyaza, "Well, what is your answer?"

Shamyaza firmly took hold of Lilith's back, pulling her into him and prompting her movement upon his firmness. Understanding his answer, Lilith complied with his unspoken request.

"It is true that I found delight in the Earth woman. Equally, I fear the loss of your warmth more than being exiled. My dear lover, please bring me to completion, for tonight I swear allegiance to both you and Satan," Shamyaza answered.

After Lilith had brought Shamyaza and herself to completion, she collapsed from exhaustion on top of her lover's body and thought once more, *Yes, my body does indeed possess the power to grant my every wish.*

The following evening, Shamyaza and his closest officers gathered to consume wine, and Lilith, with the aid of Jezebel, assembled a host of beautiful women to entertain them. Lilith adorned them with tempting apparel while Jezebel taught them the art of seduction.

Shamyaza commented to Azazel, his Chief Officer of Security, "Have you noticed the allure of the Earth women?"

Azazel scanned his surroundings and saw nothing but provocatively dressed women as far as his eyes could see. They were loose and suggestive in their ways, which pleased him greatly. "I have, Shamyaza. It is truly a pity that we are denied such pleasures," he answered.

"We do not have to concede to such tyranny, for a plan has been set to defy this cruel mandate," Shamyaza responded.

"Is this so?" Azazel asked.

"It is true what I speak, my dear comrade, for Satan and Lilith have prepared an exceptional plan of rebellion."

Azazel considered the strikingly beautiful women of Earth, observing how enamored his subordinates were with their comeliness. It was not hard for Azazel to arrive at a decision.

"My men and I will pledge allegiance to this liberation. Yet I fear that perhaps it will be me alone that enters the Earth women. Tomorrow morning, let us meet on the peak of Mt. Hermon, where we shall take an oath of allegiance. And swear before our Mother our intent to take the women of Earth for wives," Azazel proposed.

"So it shall be, my dear comrade, so it shall be," Shamyaza replied.

It was a beautiful summer day on the majestic mountaintop of Mt. Hermon. Once the watchers had assembled for this momentous occasion, Satan, with Lilith at his side, began to speak.

"My dear comrades, it pleases me to see you all in attendance for such a noble undertaking. Lilith and I have been punished for a simple act of love. This tyranny cannot be allowed to continue.

"We as gods should not be denied such pleasures as the mortals so willingly provide. However, this rebellion is not only for our benefit but theirs as well. Anu has mandated that they remain in the darkness of ignorance. These mortals are not only the creation but children of Lilith and I, which in turn, my dear comrades, makes them yours as well.

"I ask of you, what father allows their children to walk aimlessly through the wilderness? The answer is simple. There is not one among you that would do such a thing.

"We have no choice but to bring our children into the light. We must accelerate their capacity for understanding by increasing their divine DNA. It is imperative that we enter the Earth women and sow our seeds. In doing so, our number shall increase, and we shall take Heaven by force."

Satan then directed his attention to the seven officers under Shamyaza's command.

"Azazel, you shall be tasked with teaching men how to make weapons. And instruct women on how to devise seductive ornaments, and the art of applying cosmetics. Armaros, you will be tasked with teaching the mortals the resolving of enchantments and the casting of spells. Baraqel, you will teach the mortals astrology. Chazaqiel, you shall be tasked with teaching the science of meteorology. Penemuel, you will teach the art of writing with ink and paper. Sariel, you shall be tasked with teaching the courses of the moon and tidal influences, and, Shamsiel, you will teach the mortals the signs of the sun."

Satan proceeded to address all in attendance. "My brothers, how good it is, how pleasant, where the people dwell as one! Like precious ointment on the head running down upon the beard of our dear brother, upon the collar of his robe. Like the dew of Mt. Hermon coming down upon the mountains of Zion. For it is here where we shall command the blessing, life forever more!"

In unison, the watchers yelled, "Life forever more!"

Satan continued, "The sun is east in the sky. It is customary for us to kneel facing this most benevolent celestial body, in respect for Anu. Let those who wish to rebel against all forms of tyranny do so by refusing to kneel today, tomorrow, and forever."

None of the watchers kneeled. Following Satan's prompting, they all raised their left hand in a show of unity.

"Let this be regarded as a pact amongst us. Without remorse, we shall enter the Earth women and take who we will for wives. We shall take Heaven by force by creating Heaven on Earth," Satan proclaimed.

The watchers immediately began to descend Mt. Hermon in search of wives. Lilith and Satan remained atop the mountain looking down on the Earth women soon to be taken by the gods.

"My dear husband, the one whom I love the most, please observe the gift of our Mother, for one thought can change the entire universe, if impregnated in the womb of the feminine," Lilith proclaimed.

s Satan had promised, Jezebel reigned as queen for over thirty years. During this time, King Ahab, her husband, implemented the worship of Baal under Jezebel's guidance. While Jezebel understood the energies of Baal, the masses were left to believe in his physical being. Elijah, a prophet of Jehovah, was concerned with the rising popularity of Baal, which threatened his livelihood of receiving tithes. A practice Jehovah had initiated in return for Elijah's and the other rabbis' loyalty.

"Elijah, I am not pleased with the Queen of Tyre. She is turning her people away from me," Jehovah said.

"Yes, my lord, I know, and it's affecting the tithes I should receive," Elijah replied.

"My brother's prophet must be stopped. Speak with Jehu, for he is a commander in Jezebel's army who wishes to dethrone her. When this is over, I want her to be fed to the dogs," Jehovah demanded.

Elijah left at once to do Jehovah's bidding, meeting with Jehu at an inn in Judea. Jehu was unhappy with Jezebel's reluctance to promote him and often frequented the inn to indulge in wine in his anger.

Jezebel doesn't believe I'm worthy of promotion. The worship of Baal has affected her thinking. Our neighboring countries are rich with gold, yet she refuses to conquer them and gain their wealth. Sidonia needs a leader that isn't afraid to conquer and pillage—

"Hello, my dear friend," Elijah said, interrupting Jehu's thoughts.

"Hello, Elijah. What brings you here?" Jehu asked.

"I have come to deliver a message from the most high, for Jehovah is aware of your discontent for Jezebel. Her people's worship of Baal deeply troubles him, for you know he is a jealous god, and there is none above him."

"Yes, I do not feel she is worthy to rule my people. For she is a woman, weak in mind and body, and our kingdom suffers from her disdain for war. Tell me, my friend, what is the message?" Jehu asked.

"Jehovah has decreed if you dethrone Jezebel and feed her to the dogs, he shall place you upon her throne and untold riches shall be yours. There will be no enemy you cannot defeat," Elijah lied.

"Then so it shall be, my friend. I shall personally feed Jezebel to the dogs," Jehu replied.

Jehu met with his loyal subordinates, who were equally unhappy with Jezebel's refusal of their war plans. Jehu, along with 52,000 soldiers, fled to Syria to help mount an attack on Jezebel's kingdom.

Jezebel was aware of Jehu's defection and his intention to invade. Looking out her palace window, she saw Jehu's army descending upon her kingdom.

The hounds of hell approach, with greed and envy in their hearts. Fools they are. Do they not know their fate shall be seven-fold worse? I shall take pity on them, for they know not what they do. Their belief in finality makes them no better than the beasts of the fields. Their feeble minds seek my undoing, and they can kill my body, but I am not a body but an idea, a thought that is immortal, without a beginning or ending. Jehu shall see a woman with no fear of death, unlike anything he has ever seen on a battleground. I shall prepare to die with the dignity of a queen, Jezebel thought.

She then proceeded to dress herself in her finest dress and applied lipstick before lying on her plush bed. She poured a glass of wine and waited Jehu's arrival.

Suddenly there was a loud bang from her bedroom doors being kicked open and Jehu walked into Jezebel's room with a sword in his hand.

"Is it peace, Zimri, murderer of your master?" Jezebel asked, invoking the name of the man who had ruled but seven days after seizing the throne from his king.

Angered by Jezebel's words, Jehu looked at her eunuchs and asked, "Who is on my side?"

Fearing death, the eunuchs threw Jezebel out the window to her death, where wild dogs began to eat her dead body.

Jehu them placed himself upon her throne and commenced to rule her kingdom.

News of Jezebel's death travelled quickly throughout the region, and when Nephthys learned of Jezebel's doom, she immediately set course for Babylon to inform Lilith of the dreadful news.

"My dear sister, I have a most terrible message I must report to you," Nephthys lamented.

"Waste no time, my dear sister—tell me," Lilith demanded.

"It is Jezebel—she has met a horrible fate, for Jehovah's prophet has had her killed. And her body was fed to the dogs."

"What, who is responsible for this!" Lilith cried.

"He is known as Jehu, and he now sits on Jezebel's throne. He was angered by her distaste for war and does not view women as equal to men. He believes we are weak and cannot rule, and has implemented laws forbidding women from any official government offices," Nephthys replied.

"The human males are disgusting in their thoughts. They oppress the very ones who are responsible for their existence. Even the lion, the king of the jungle, has great reverence for the lioness. I shall deal with this Jehu and his male son, for his time on Earth is limited. However, I shall not put one hand on him," Lilith decreed.

Jehu had become drunk with power after ascending to the throne. He'd had many of Jezebel's loyal servants, priests, and priestesses executed, and forbidden the worship of Baal. He'd also had the most beautiful virgins rounded up throughout the kingdom to be his concubines.

One night, as Jehu fell asleep surrounded by his many lovers, he had a dream. Standing in a dark room, Jehu heard the voice of a woman repeatedly calling his name.

Jehu, Jehu...

Jehu, your lover awaits you.

Flashes of light surrounded Jehu, illuminating the face of the most beautiful woman he had ever seen. Her voice was comforting and sensual.

Suddenly, a door made of grey mist appeared before him and the woman walked through it wearing nothing but a short scarlet wraparound skirt. Her hair was the color of fire and she had dark yellow eyes. She was holding an owl in one hand and a golden chalice in the other. Caressing the owl with her hand, Lilith whispered to it, *Go and rest at the window. Watch as Jehu learns the power of a woman.*

The owl did as she commanded. Lilith than discarded her skirt, exposing her purple panties.

Jehu, lie on the bed.

Seductively, she slid her panties down her legs, climbed atop Jehu, and guided his firmness into her.

Jehu, remember the owl, for it is all-seeing.

My purple panties represent my rule over you.

My golden chalice is full of many abominations of which you are currently getting drunk on.

When Jehu awoke from his sleep, he found his bed was wet from the essence he had released while asleep.

He was startled to see an owl at the same window Jezebel had been thrown from. Startled, confused, and fearful, he frantically rose from the bed. His lovers awoke from all the commotion, and Jehu noticed they were all wearing purple panties.

"What sorcery is this?" he screamed.

Fearing his lovers were demonic witches, he ordered them to be killed, but Jehu was unable to get Lilith out of his mind. He feared her words and revelations. At the same time, he was madly in love with her beauty. He barricaded himself within the palace walls, slowly going insane over the months that followed. When the time came for him to go to battle, he was unable to perform—every face of the enemy was Lilith's. Jehu was captured on the battleground. His enemies cut off his head and fed his dead body to the lions where all of Sidonia could bear witness.

Lilith entertained many a mortal in the room of pleasure, but there were none among the men of Earth she prized more than Joseph, who had unknowingly inspired the great rebellion. Although Lilith loved Joseph intensely, she never allowed him to mount her. The ways of the goddess forbid any but her husband to do so, and yet, the thought of it had always secretly intrigued her.

Understanding that Jehovah had employed psychological warfare on an inferior race of beings, Lilith knew it was only logical that the same approach would be needed to undo the damage caused—but now it would be done with love and harm to none. *Yes, you must be as wise as a serpent and harmless as a dove*, Lilith thought.

Jehovah had set himself up as the one true god, so the mortals needed a viable alternative. More importantly, this alternative would need to be one of them. A genetic upgrade would be needed to accomplish this, requiring both a god and goddess to procreate with mortals under favorable conditions to produce a male and a female. A goddess who allowed a mortal to impregnate her would almost certainly be considered shameful among the watchers. Being the only goddess on Earth who pleased herself with mortal flesh placed Lilith first and foremost in this unenviable yet fascinating role.

If Lilith's plans were to come to fruition, it would need to be she that allowed a mortal's seed to infiltrate her divine womb. And with great certainty, for ages to come, she would be crucified with considerable degradation.

To further complicate matters, to ensure impregnation, Lilith would need to allow a mortal to mount her. She contemplated long on how her husband would take such a suggestion. Satan was aware of all Lilith's lovers, as she was his. He also knew Lilith favored Joseph the most among the men of Earth.

Surely my husband must know that I love none more than him, regardless of how many times I have pleased myself with Joseph? I have always followed the customs of the goddess. And while it's true Joseph satisfies me greatly, it is not his seed touching my creative womb that disgusts me. Knowing that I will find pleasure in allowing Joseph to mount me is what truly disgusts me, Lilith thought.

Unlike the gods, the mortals had a blurry idea of what love was—they had difficulty understanding this most powerful non-restrictive force. The open promiscuity of the gods was not practiced by the men and women of Earth. This self-imposed inhibition had emerged from Jehovah's absurd religious propaganda. Lilith and Satan found it mildly amusing that the mortals they had taken for lovers hid those liaisons from their spouses. Even so, they never infringed upon their silly hypocritical views.

One day Lilith complained to Satan that Joseph couldn't properly please her due to his wife Mary's lonesomeness—it demanded much of Joseph's time and was the source of his hurried performances.

"My dear husband, Joseph's wife's name is Mary. She is pleasing to the eye. Please lie with her so that her loneliness will no longer impede my pleasures," Lilith begged.

"My dear wife, I shall find Mary and take her as one of my lovers," he responded.

"I greatly appreciate your assistance, but there is something of greater importance that I must discuss with you. Our brother has infected the minds of the mortals with religion. They need a savior, and it is us who must heed this call," Lilith solemnly stated.

"What is it that you propose, my dear wife?"

"You must impregnate Mary, and I pray that you do not find me shameful, but Joseph must impregnate me as well."

As Satan stood facing Lilith in a state of shock, she continued, "I must give birth to the message. You, my dear husband, must give life to the messenger. I do not see any other way to effectively undo the wrongs of our brother."

Lilith did not wish to confess how much she desired the forbidden act of allowing Joseph, a mere mortal, to mount her. And so she deceived Satan.

"My dear husband, you know that I find pleasure with Joseph, but the very thought of him mounting me brings me great disgust. Allowing him to release his essence in me will surely bring much anguish, so it is only for our cause that I have suggested such an act," Lilith said.

She began to cry from the shame of her lies. Yet her desire to allow the forbidden was great, and so she continued to lie. "There is none worthy to mount me but you, my dear husband. It is only for the love of humanity and our eventual freedom that I present this option to you."

Understanding both the logic and seriousness of Lilith's plan, Satan gave her his blessing.

In order to determine the most optimum time for impregnation, as well as the desired gender, Satan and Lilith applied the science of astrology.

As only it could be, Lilith was to give birth to a female. The male child who would serve the goddess was to sprout forth from the womb of Mary. It was ascertained that the act of impregnation should occur on a Friday evening, with the sun in the ninth house, while Mercury passed through the twins. To ensure Lilith's fertilization, Joseph would need to release his essence into her not once but twice.

The evening of the conception had arrived. Up until this point, Lilith had always used some form of contraceptive with her lovers. Tonight, however, would be different. The mortals had never been educated in matters of birth control. As such, Lilith found no reason to explain to Joseph such matters.

Lilith and Satan debated long and hard whether to inform Mary of her pending impregnation. It was their contention that the mortals had grown accustomed to deception—they would not be good teachers if they didn't allow for lessons to be learned. And so they planned to proceed without making Mary aware of their plan.

Lilith requested that Satan lie with Mary first. As she put it, "I will need you by my side after suffering the indignity of allowing Joseph to mount me."

Upon being summoned, Mary quickly arrived at the room of pleasure. Within minutes of undressing, Satan ejaculated his essence into her. Then, knowing that Lilith would soon need to summon Joseph, he directed Mary to promptly dress and return to her house.

After Mary's departure, Satan entered their living quarters to find Lilith wearing a provocative outfit that clung to her well-toned body. As if she feared what he would think of this, she quickly said, "My attire is so because I wish to arouse Joseph so that my agony of being mounted by him is brief. I have summoned Joseph, and he shall arrive soon."

With a sense of urgency, and a degree of enthusiasm, Lilith hastily headed to the room of pleasure to await Joseph's arrival. Satan noticed that her demeanor was not that of a woman in anguish of what she was soon to do but rather that of someone eagerly anticipating the act she was soon to carry out.

When Lilith heard Joseph's knock on the door, she was overcome by her desire to allow her lover the forbidden.

I feel shameful. Yet I long for Joseph to please me. I pray if my husband is to learn of my true desire that he will forgive me, for I have wanted this from the beginning with Adam. I shall not only yield to my desire, I shall take pleasure in doing so, Lilith thought before opening the door.

"Lilith, your dress has provoked me to firmness," Joseph said as he stood in the doorway, transfixed by Lilith's beauty.

"I am filled with joy that you find satisfaction in my appearance. My dress is in honor of the heavenly experience we shall share tonight, for I am equally enamored by your strong physique. It surely brings moisture to my garden.

"Let us waste no time. Undress so I can take delight in you," Lilith said as she began to take off her dress.

While Joseph undressed, Lilith climbed onto the bed and lay flat on her back. This unusual act confused Joseph—he stood mystified at the end of the bed.

"My dear lover, for tonight I shall allow the forbidden," Lilith declared as she invitingly spread her legs.

"My dear goddess, I fear that I know of your desire. Surely your husband shall kill me for such treachery," Joseph contested.

"Calm yourself, Joseph—you are right in knowing my desire, but I assure you that my husband is aware of what I want and has given his blessing," Lilith reassured him.

Reaching out with her hand, Lilith said, "Come please me in this way, for I have secretly craved this from the beginning."

Overcome by the view of Lilith's exposed garden, Joseph climbed onto the bed between Lilith's legs and hastily guided his member to her entrance.

The feel of her lover's body on hers, along with the anticipation of Joseph entering her in this way, excited Lilith. Yet the moment Joseph thrust his member deep inside her, Lilith thought of how she had deceived her husband, closed her eyes, and shamefully turned her head to the side.

Though she tried, Lilith couldn't resist the pleasure Joseph was giving her. It humiliated her to find delight in each forceful thrust, yet being dominated in this way excited her greatly. She felt degraded, lying there with her legs spread, and yet she spread them wider, yielding to her lover.

Although filled with remorse for deceiving Satan, she moaned with pleasure—allowing Joseph, a mere mortal, to debase her body as if she was a common whore brought Lilith great liberation.

After Joseph's completion, she ran to the restroom as tears fell down her cheeks. Confused by her feelings of shame, Lilith wiped away her tears and began to reapply her cosmetics, before walking out of the restroom to receive Joseph's essence again.

She stood at the door in deep contemplation.

I have just allowed a mortal to perform the forbidden, yet I was neither repulsed nor disgusted. On the contrary, I found it quite pleasing. As all things that are done in the dark must ultimately come to the light, I shall make my husband aware of my trickery. I will speak truth concerning the pleasures Joseph has given me and, more importantly, my desire for the forbidden.

It is true that I require Joseph to mount me once more. This I shall do. However, I shall not stop there, for I shall relish the feel of Joseph's body atop mine till I am forced to return to my dear husband, Lilith thought.

Nearly three hours later, Lilith left the room of pleasure. When she entered her living quarters. Satan facetiously asked, "For an act that was to bring such anguish, I wonder why my dear wife has entertained Joseph till this hour."

"My dear husband, I must speak the truth. I pray that you will forgive my deceptive ways. I was not disgusted by the thought of Joseph mounting me. The truth is I have long desired it.

"In the beginning, my shame brought me to tears. But the pleasure was more than I could bear, and I quickly succumbed to it. I ask that you forgive my lustful ways. But I shall allow the forbidden again, for it is a pleasure I cannot, and will not, deny myself.

"My dear husband, there are none whom I love more than you. For you are my brother, my lover, and together we are one. I have already shamed myself in the eyes of the gods, yet I am shameless. For these reasons, I ask that you overlook my past transgressions and condone my future ones," Lilith replied.

"My dear Lilith, I am disappointed with your deceptive ways. However, I am inspired by your truth. I shall not fault you for your desires or actions, for it would be illogical to deny such pleasures to the one I love most. My dear wife, I will overlook your past actions and condone your future ones. I only ask that you restrain yourself in your deceitful ways. As for forgiving you, that is something I cannot do, my love. Simply because in my eyes you have done no wrong," Satan answered.

The medical officers of the watchers administered pregnancy tests to both Lilith and Mary. As expected, the results were positive. Lilith's meticulous preparations had paid off. She had successfully conceived a female child and Mary a male child.

Immediately, Satan summoned Mary. Upon her arrival, he couldn't help but notice the light of her persona—the illuminated lifeforce that all Earth women with child exhibited.

"Mary, please sit down. I must talk with you about matters of great importance," Satan said.

"Yes, Lord Satan, please do inform me of such things," Mary replied.

"As you know, Mary, after I first entered you, you had a great fear of conceiving a child with me, for Joseph still considers you to be a virgin. I told you that there was nothing to fear. I did not lie; however, this is not true of our last liaison."

"Whatever do you mean?" Mary asked.

"When we last pleased each other, I did not take the necessary precautions. As a result of this, you are with child."

"No, Satan, please tell me this isn't so! What shall I tell Joseph? Surely he shall divorce me for such a shameful act, condemning me to wander the Earth as an adulteress," Mary cried.

Having little pity for her deceptive ways, Satan replied, "Perhaps, Mary, you should tell Joseph the truth. For the truth shall set you free."

Mary sat on the bed and began to cry. Sitting next to her, Satan explained the purpose of her pregnancy in so much as her mortal ears could hear. With great pride, he spoke of their future seed, who would be the bright morning star; his only begotten son who was to save Earth from the tyrannical rule of Jehovah—the one who would be called Emmanuel.

"My dear lover, I now better understand the measure of your ways. I shall confess to Joseph the truth of our love—a love that I am not willing to abandon. As you allow Lilith to lie with others, so shall Joseph be required to permit me," Mary affirmed.

When Mary revealed her pregnancy to Joseph, along with her intention to remain Satan's lover, Joseph yelled out in anger, "You have brought great shame upon me by committing such a sinful act! For it is true that I love you, but I cannot possibly condone your wicked ways."

"My dear husband, you have said that you love me, have you not?" Mary seductively asked.

"Yes, this is true, but you are now an adulteress. Since you are now with child, I am unable to discreetly forgive you, for the townspeople know that I have yet to enter you. I have no other choice but to divorce you."

"My dear husband, I am filled with great remorse for bringing shame upon you. I pray that before I am sent to wander the Earth as an adulteress, you permit me to show you one of the many secrets of the gods that I now have knowledge of."

"What is this knowledge you speak of, woman?" Joseph asked.

"I am unable to tell you. I can only show you," Mary answered.

"Very well. I shall permit this before you are to be sent into the wilderness."

Mary instantly dropped to her knees in front of Joseph. Exposing his sex organ, she began to caress it with her tongue until it was fully erect. She then took his member into her mouth, until she had efficiently released his essence, as she had done so many times for Satan.

Mary rose from her knees, wiping his essence from her lips, and asked teasingly, "Is it still your desire for me to leave? For that is just one of many secrets I have learned."

Having just been pleasured in a way he had never experienced or known of, Joseph replied in bewilderment, "No, Mary, for this is no longer my wish. You have taught me a secret of the gods. There is no other who can show me such things."

"Joseph, I will indeed remain your wife, but as Satan permits Lilith to lie with others, I shall require that you permit the same for me," Mary insisted.

"I shall gladly submit myself to this stipulation, but what shall we tell the townspeople? For they know I have yet to enter you?" Joseph asked.

After Mary had explained to Joseph the predestined role of the child she carried, she said, "We shall tell the townspeople that I am still a virgin, that I have not defiled the house of Joseph by committing adultery, but rather God himself impregnated me in order to bring forth a savior. One who will redeem humanity from their sinful ways."

The plan Lilith had devised was working flawlessly. She gave birth to a daughter whom she named Mary Magdalene. Shortly thereafter, Mary gave birth to a son whom she named Jesus.

Jesus was a mischievous child, endowed with abilities other children his age did not possess, which he often utilized in less than becoming ways. However, as was expected, he matured rapidly. By the age of twelve, he was teaching the rabbis of Nazareth. Upon his fourteenth birthday, Jesus observed the custom of those who had come before him. As had been done with his forefather Abraham, he was sent to Egypt in order to learn the Ancient Egyptian Mystery Systems.

Compared to Jesus, Mary Magdalene was an extremely well-mannered child and had a deep-rooted bond with her mother. Wherever Lilith was, Mary Magdalene was sure to be nearby. What intrigued both Lilith and Satan was the effect she had upon Jesus. From his mischievous youth through to his regal years of teaching the rabbis, they often observed as he sat quietly next to Mary Magdalene, listening intently as she ministered to him. For this was truly Mary Magdalene's purpose for being, and it was astonishing the way in which Jesus inherently knew who his teacher was, for the blood of the goddess literally flowed through her veins.

An essential aspect of Lilith's plan was the arranged marriage of Jesus and Mary. As a result of this, it was mandated that they grow up together, and thus they shared more of a sibling relationship.

At the age of eighteen, the spirit led Mary into the wilderness to be tempted by the Adversary, where she fasted for forty days and forty nights. Afterwards, she was hungry.

The Tempter approached her and said, "If you are truly a goddess, command that these stones become loaves of bread."

"It is written that one does not live by bread alone but by the purpose of one's life," Mary replied.

Then the Tempter took her to the holy city and made her stand on the wall of the temple, and said, "If you are truly a goddess, throw yourself down, for it is written that the elemental energies are at your disposal."

"It is not for you to put the goddess to the test," Mary replied.

Then the Tempter took her to a high mountain. He showed her all the kingdoms of the world. "I shall give you all that you see, if you will bow and worship me," the Tempter offered.

"Flee from me, Tempter, for you cannot give me what is already mine," Mary replied.

Immediately, the Adversary fled, and Melchizedek came to minister to Mary Magdalene.

When Mary returned from the wilderness, she sought out her mother. She found her standing outside the temple.

With a warm, maternal smile, Lilith embraced Mary. "I have been expecting you," she said.

"Yes, I felt your energy beckon me," Mary replied.

"Mary, before we enter the temple, I wish you to read the sign above the doors."

"The sign reads, *Know thyself. Let all who enter leave all hope behind*," Mary read aloud.

"Do you understand the meaning?" Lilith asked.

"I understand the importance of knowing thyself, for without that, there can be no progress of any kind. But I do not understand why one would wish to leave such a beautiful thing as hope behind."

"My dear child, hope is only good for those that do not know. Knowing is much better than hoping, for in hoping one becomes like a log being tossed about at the current's discretion. Follow me inside, for the time has come for you to learn the ways of the goddess," Lilith said.

Lilith guided Mary into the inner sanctuary and through a door behind the altar, which led into a secret room reserved for initiatory purposes. There was a golden statue in the corner of the room depicting a mother holding her child. Decorating the walls were paintings of the sun and moon, and various astrological themes including the wheel of destiny. There was nothing else in the room except two chairs, situated in the middle of the room, directly under a ceiling painting of the constellation Orion.

"Mary, there are only two chairs here, as knowledge is only passed from one mouth to one ear, for wisdom cannot be dispensed to all. Those that have been tested and found worthy shall know. All others shall have such things concealed from them, for those who have charitable hearts and commit silent acts of love shall know all things," Lilith said.

Lilith instructed Mary to sit and began to minister. "I am the mistress of the nine major gods. The lady of all, the woman who lightens darkness. The time has now arrived for you to be brought to the awareness of your true essence.

"There was never a time when woman was not. It is well known that a man comes from a woman, yet the origin of the woman is unknown. Without a man, she produced a man. And it is for this reason that the man who knows her has conceded on bended knee that he is the son of a widow. She is the first thought, the image of spirit. She became the universal womb, for she precedes everything.

"The universe is the result of the male and female energy source—the harmonious union of these two perfect opposites, which are equal in strength and present in everything. The human male is repressive and hypocritical in nature. It is imperative that you shed these archaic burdens and allow them to die a glorious death by reclaiming your sovereignty from the grips of superstitious and profane men; by using the very power inherent within you, sexual domination. Religious imposters and various other kings of this world are aware of women's seductive powers and have worked hard to suppress them. But to no avail, for even King Solomon in all his glory fell victim to a woman.

"Understanding the energies that your body produces within men will have the world at your fingertips. In this physical plane of existence, everything is vibrating with energy. The higher the vibration, the more potent this force becomes, yet its visibility decreases. However, there is one constant that prevails throughout the universe: to achieve greatness, one must be willing to let go of greatness, for wealth and power are but an earthly illusion. True power can come only through a pure heart," Lilith taught.

Lilith then stood and hugged Mary. And as a loving mother who is proud of their child, she shed tears of joy.

After hearing her divine instructions, Mary promptly set out to find Jesus. She discovered him sitting under a fig tree, motionless, in a state of deep contemplation.

"Jesus, you appear troubled—what are your thoughts?" Mary asked.

"I have had a dream yet the interpretation has not revealed itself," Jesus answered.

"Speak of your dream, for I shall bring the revelation," Mary replied.

"I was attempting to pass through the door of the great temple of knowledge. However, on each side of the temple door lay two ferocious lions. These beasts were double the size of any lion I have seen. Their appearance stirred fear within me. They rose and walked towards me, and so I ran to safety. I was troubled, for how could I pass with these beasts guarding the entrance? But my desire for knowledge was overwhelming. I decided that I would attempt to pass, even if it meant certain death.

"When I approached the temple, the lions rose once again and walked towards me. This time I was without fear. They stood one on each side of me, walking with me as I entered the temple. I do not understand the nature of this dream," Jesus said.

"It is a blessing to my soul to hear of your courage in such a critical test," Mary jubilantly shouted.

"I am confused—of what test do you speak?" Jesus asked.

"It is a confirmation of your worthiness to be my messenger, in which fear cannot exist, for I shall send you out like a sheep amongst wolves. Therefore, you must be as shrewd as a snake, yet as peaceful as a dove.

"In the beginning of your dream, you had great fear of those majestic beasts. Then you conquered this most evil emotion, for the beasts were not guarding the temple door but you," Mary revealed.

"Why do they guard me?" Jesus asked.

"You have been chosen to deliver the people from the tyrannical grip of Jehovah, for you will show them the path to divinity, which is: in the beginning was the word, and the word was with God, and the word is God. You shall teach them that no one can come to me unless the Mother who sent me brings them near. And I shall raise them on their last day.

"You shall cure their disease of greed and lack. The Mother will know when she is hungry and not fed; when she is thirsty and given nothing to drink; when she is a stranger yet not invited in; when she is in need of clothes and not clothed; when she is sick and in prison and not looked after, for whatever one does not do for the least of humanity, they do not do for her.

"For the people have been taught an eye for an eye, and a tooth for a tooth, but salvation requires resisting the evil one. But this is not to suppose you are to bring peace. No, you shall not be sent out amongst them with peace but with a sword," Mary concluded.

"And how will I know who is worthy of this divine knowledge?" Jesus asked.

"A good tree cannot bear bad fruit; nor can a bad tree bear good fruit. Every tree that bears undesirable fruit is cut down and thrown into the fire. Therefore, by their fruits, you will know them," Mary declared.

"And what of your message is the most important that I shall impart?" Jesus asked.

"It is one of faith, hope, and charity, but of these three, the greatest is charity," Mary answered.

Mary Magdalene took Jesus for a husband at the age of twenty-one. In preparation for spreading the message, she selected twelve worthy female disciples and directed Jesus to select twelve worthy males to be his.

The religions of Jehovah were divisive and barbaric. It was the mission of Jesus and Mary to replace the practice of an eye for an eye with the practice of loving one's enemy; substituting blood sacrifices with prayers rooted in action; eliminating war while instituting peace.

There was one element of Jehovah's wickedness that couldn't be disrupted in that age, which was the heinous act of establishing the male energy force as the one true God. In Heaven as well as throughout the cosmos, it was known that the female energy source was the mother of all, and therefore God. By creating a religion that lacked this necessary element, Jehovah had single-handedly placed Earth into chaos, for there could be no harmony within the spheres of existence without a creative womb to produce such an agreement.

Thus it was decreed from the beginning that while Jesus in fact would be following the guidance of Mary, to the masses he would be presented as the savior of humanity. In that day and age, the men and, sadly, the women would not have accepted Mary for who and what she was.

In order to fund her ministry, Mary initiated a chosen few into the most ancient Order of the Temple Prostitutes. The divine prostitutes among Mary's disciples not only earned the necessary funds to finance Lilith's objective, they managed those funds as well—their acts of love more effective than any sword could have been.

It pleased Lilith and Satan to see Jesus and Mary's concept of free love—it was equal to that of the gods. It was refreshing to see two mortals who didn't view love as restrictive and possessive. This sentiment rang loud throughout the universe—when love was regulated, it would flee to become one again with its true source, which was freedom.

They took on many lovers for themselves. Mary found favor in the harbinger of Jesus called John the Baptist, while Jesus favored Salome, one of Mary's disciples, whom Mary had initiated into the ancient Order of the Temple Prostitutes. Salome was an adept in ritualistic sex and erotic dance.

During this period, the inhabitants of Earth were mainly ignorant and simple-minded. However, a few had been received into the mysteries. As such, their paths were illuminated, and their ways were ritualistic.

One day, Jesus left Cana to enter into Nain. There were a great multiple of loyal followers, as well as the curious, who gathered to see and listen to Jesus preach.

As Jesus and his disciples entered the city gates, their path was obstructed by a funeral procession for the son of a widow.

When the funeral procession neared Jesus and his disciples, Jesus recognized the widow and her son. The widow knew Jesus by the secrets he displayed. Honoring the master in her presence, she beseeched Jesus to raise her son from the gates of death.

Upon observing the rite being properly performed, Jesus told the widow, "Do not weep, for your son only sleeps."

With a strong grip, Jesus took the young man by the hand and said, "Awake from your sleep and arise. Place your trust in God, and, with no fear, follow your guide."

The dead man immediately came back to life and began to speak. The multiple were overcome by fear. They fell to their knees in prayer after witnessing what they perceived to be a miracle. Jesus was unable to remedy their confusion, so he allowed them to remain in their self-imposed hell, for one should never cast their pearls unto the swine.

I n the city of Jerusalem lived Hildana, the wife of Sanhedrin. She was a beautiful young woman whose husband forced her to earn their living by selling her body. Sanhedrin had been a source of trouble for Jesus throughout his youth. He yearned for the attention of Mary Magdalene and resented how she openly showed Jesus affection. This envy followed Sanhedrin even to his adult years.

When Sanhedrin learned Jesus had returned to Jerusalem, he set out to assist the Scribes and Pharisees in arresting him. The religious zealots of the day feared the popularity of Jesus greatly; Mary Magdalene's ministry had exposed their flaws and ignorance in many matters.

Sanhedrin brought his wife to the feast at Jerusalem and ordered her to prostitute. While Hildana was pleasing one of the men at the feast, Sanhedrin betrayed his wife—he gathered the Jewish rulers and brought them to witness his wife's illicit acts.

"I have caught my wife in the act of adultery. By the law of Moses, she should be stoned to death," Sanhedrin told the Pharisees.

Sanhedrin knew that the Pharisees would ask Jesus how they should handle such a matter. The law of Moses decreed that Hildana should be stoned to death; however, the Roman rulers had denied the Jews this without their approval. Sanhedrin, as well as the Pharisees, knew that regardless of how Jesus answered, he would be considered wrong, and they hoped to use his statement to justify his arrest.

The Scribes and the Pharisees apprehended Hildana and made her stand in the middle of the crowd. They asked Jesus, "Master, this woman was caught in the act of adultery. Moses commanded us to stone such a woman. So what do you say?"

Jesus bent down and drew a circle in the sand with his finger. They continued to ask him. Jesus rose to his feet and said, "Let the one who is without sin throw the first stone."

One by one, they dropped their stones and walked away, until Jesus stood alone with Hildana.

"Woman, where are your accusers? Has not one man condemned you?" Jesus asked.

"Not one man, master," Hildana answered.

"Neither shall I, for one shall be judged by the measure that one judges. Go, for you have done no wrong," Jesus replied.

Hildana forsook her husband and became a disciple of Mary. Salome later initiated Hildana into the ancient Order of the Temple Prostitutes.

Martha was informed by her friends that Jesus was drawing near to Bethany. She hastily set out to greet him.

"Master, when you were last here, my brother Lazarus was but a child. He is now a man, yet he is blinded and dead."

Mary, Martha's sister, had given up all hope for Lazarus, but Martha had faith that the master could raise her brother from his ignorance.

"Master, Lazarus is worthy and well qualified. His charitable acts are many. He seeks the light, but his deathly ways prevent him from understanding the light. He has no time for the words of a woman. I beg of you to forgive his disrespect. My brother is dead and unaware of himself. Yet I know you can bring life to him," Martha implored.

"Martha, man comes through the womb alone. For this reason, man must seek the light on his own. You cannot save your brother. It is only he who can save himself. My brothers are strong and take the noose from their own necks. Verily I say unto you, Martha, the ones that are incapable of doing so, I never knew," Jesus stated.

In time, Lazarus asked Jesus to accept him into the silent brotherhood. It pleased Jesus to see his desire to be brought back from the gates of hell on his own free will and accord. After being duly and truly prepared, Jesus received Lazarus into the silent brotherhood.

Under Mary Magdalene's guidance, Jesus traveled the land proclaiming the Gospel of Mary. He cured the sick and afflicted, and his fame grew throughout the Earth—great crowds from all corners of the planet came to follow him. Because of this, at times Jesus had difficulty remaining humble. One day, Salome overheard a private conversation between John the Baptist and Mary Magdalene.

"My dear lover, Jesus has done many great things and has followed your counsel well. But I fear that he has become the message, leaving the messenger behind," John said.

"I am aware of my husband's shortcomings, but such is expected from the male energy source. However, what you have said is true, and I am gravely concerned," Mary replied.

"Your wisdom must be transmitted free from the destructive energies of the ego. Allow me, your humble lover, to assume the duties of your teachings," John pleaded.

"My dear lover, I have heard your request and shall consider it," Mary replied.

Upon hearing this, Salome immediately sought the advice of her mother Herodias, who was the wife of Philip, the brother of King Herod. Herodias was having an affair with King Herod. John the Baptist had told Herod that it was unlawful for him to enter Herodias, and seeing an opportunity to rid herself of the Baptist, Herodias crafted a cunning plan: she would have King Herod arrest John for interfering with her pleasures.

At a birthday celebration for King Herod, Herodias put her plan into effect.

"Salome, it is the king's birthday. There are none who are equal in your dancing abilities. Dance for him, for when he sees the rhythm of your body, he shall surely desire to enter into you and be willing to grant your every wish," Herodias said.

Without delay, Salome dressed in her seductive dancing garments and approached the king.

"My king, I wish to celebrate your birthday with a dance. Allow me to please your eyes with the rhythm of my body," Salome propositioned.

Upon seeing Salome's alluring curves, the king was instantly aroused. "My dear, I will find delight in granting your request. Yes, allow my eyes the pleasure of your view," he replied.

Once Salome had finished dancing, King Herod, enchanted by the charms of her body, said, "My dear, I find great delight in the rhythm of your body. Allow me to lie with you and I shall grant whatever you ask of me. I will even give you half of my kingdom."

"I will allow you to enter me, but I want the head of John the Baptist on a silver platter immediately," Salome said.

King Herod promptly ordered the executioner to behead the Baptist. He brought the head to Salome on a silver platter; Salome then followed the king to his quarters to uphold her end of the agreement.

The news of John's beheading brought great sorrow to Mary Magdalene, and disappointment filled her heart upon learning of her disciple's request. With no thoughts of vengeance, she simply forgave Salome, yet while Mary knew that her husband had nothing to do with Salome's morbid petition to King Herod, she was keenly aware that he showed no signs of grief either.

itting in a lily field, Mary thought on the negative impact of her husband's popularity.

John was right in his words. Jesus has become the message and not the messenger. The DNA-restricted humans are quick to make him a god to be worshipped. I fear the message shall be lost. While he never takes credit for his works, his love for attention is growing. Furthermore, I fear for his safety, for the people are quick to raise one but quicker to destroy one. I must talk with my mother concerning this matter immediately.

Before Mary could rise up in search of her mother, Lilith appeared.

"Mary, I sense your troubled heart. Please tell me what is distressing you?" Lilith asked.

"It is Jesus—his love of attention has become an issue. But it is his safety that worries me the most."

"Oh, Mary, it is to be expected, for the people have made him out to be one that should be worshipped. But there is no aid available for his safety," Lilith explained.

"Why is there no aid?" Mary asked.

"The messenger is always loved by the needy and despised by those corrupted by power. Kings fear him more than they do the sword of their enemies. To hold on to their illusion of control, they seek to silence the messenger. However, my dear daughter, they shall both get their due reward. For as Mithras was crucified on a cross, so shall Jesus meet the same fate. But have no fear for your husband, for there is nothing permanent in either death or life. Your husband's path was decided long before his earthly existence," Lilith answered.

As the years passed, Mary Magdalene took Judas, a disciple of Jesus, as a lover. He pleased her well and was subservient to all her desires. However, Judas was unable to handle the magnetism of Mary and desired to have her all to himself.

During this time, Jehovah had prompted the chief priests to accuse Jesus of blasphemy. They directed the temple guards to locate and bring forth Jesus to answer this most serious charge.

One afternoon, as Mary was pleasing herself above Judas, he became enraged with jealousy over having to share the goddess.

"My dear lover, it is my desire to mount you," Judas boldly stated.

Mary did not stop pleasing herself but slowed her pace. Not wanting Judas in that way, she replied, with a tone of annoyance, "Judas, do not speak of such things, for you know this is forbidden."

Displeased by Mary's lack of concern, Judas replied, "Yes, Mary, I know that my desire is forbidden, but the authorities are looking for your husband—if you do not permit my request, I shall be forced to turn him in to them."

Mary did not reply to Judas's threat; nor did she stop in her indulgence. She continued until she let out a loud moan and collapsed over Judas.

Lying above him with his member still inside her, she whispered into his ear, "Judas, for your transgressions, you shall never feel my warmth again. For I say unto you: once you have done the evil you speak of, you shall surely die at the end of a rope."

Mary immediately went to inform Jesus of his disciple's intentions.

The following day, Mary arranged a dinner that would be the last Jesus had with his disciples.

With Mary seated to his right, Jesus spoke as the disciples ate. "Truthfully I say that one of you shall betray me."

And the disciples all asked, "Is it I?"

"For he that has dipped his hand in the dish shall betray me. The son of man must go as it is written of him: but woe unto that man by whom the son of man is betrayed! It would have been better for that man if he had not been born. Thirty pieces of silver is useless in the realm of the nonphysical. One never gains when they lose the virtues of their soul," Jesus answered.

The words of a goddess are law. Shortly after Judas betrayed Jesus for thirty pieces of silver, he did, in fact, die at the end of a rope. Deeply regretting what he had done, Judas returned the thirty pieces of silver to the priests—then, seeking to find relief from his guilt, he hung himself.

As Mary willed it to be, the ministry of Jesus Christ came to an end as he hung on a cross. There were many women there that day he was crucified, looking on from a distance, who had followed Jesus and ministered to him. Standing next to the cross were his mother Mary, his mother's sister Mary of Clopas, Mary Magdalene, and his beloved Salome.

As death slowly approached, Jesus saw his mother and one of his disciples. He said to his mother, "Mother, behold your son." He then told his disciple, "Behold your mother." And from that moment forward, the disciple gave aid to the widow.

Lilith and Satan stood at the riverbank, listening to Jesus's last words: "Father, forgive them, as they know not what they do."

As Satan stood there with his head down in sorrow, Lilith, with tears falling down her cheeks, said to her husband, "Your son, even facing death, has shown a pure heart, for he beseeched you to forgive their cruel acts."

"Yes indeed, he truly fulfilled his life's mission. Lilith, you must speak with your daughter at once. She must flee before she meets the same fate," Satan replied.

"That has always been her destiny, my dear husband. Mary must protect the seed of enlightenment," Lilith replied.

Lilith made her way to the cross and helped a sobbing Mary to her feet.

"My dear daughter, we must leave at once, for you carry the holy grail which must be protected. The blood that flows through your veins and your unborn child's veins shall be the light in a very dark world. It is your bloodline that will show the kingdom of Heaven to not be in any temple or church but within every worthy individual. You must travel to Egypt, where the descendants of Moses shall provide safe passage to France. Take Lazarus and his sister with you as well. Also direct the disciples of Jesus to record his works," Lilith said.

She embraced Mary and said, "Your mother is proud of you. Fear not that we shall not meet again, for we shall. But in those moments that you may feel as if you've been abandoned, know that a mother is always there in mind and/or body."

Mary Magdalene directed the disciples to write of what they had witnessed in their travels with Jesus so that future generations would be able to hear the message of enlightenment that, from under her counsel, Jesus had taught. She then fled to Southern France with her unborn baby, who would be known as Sara, along with Mary Jacobi and Mary Salome, as well as Lazarus and his sister Martha.

Mary turned her attention to her children, instructing her daughters in the ways of the goddess and initiating them into the Ancient Order of the Temple Prostitutes. There they were taught the hidden knowledge and power of the female energy source, which they and their offspring have used ever since to restore balance and harmony to the universe.

CAPE CANAVERAL, FLORIDA, 1969

The United States and Russia were in a race to be the first to the moon. In the beginning, they believed space domination would give one of the two the edge in future military operations, but NASA soon discovered from its orbital satellites numerous anomalies concerning the moon. Satellites beamed images back to Earth that appeared to show structures on the far side of the moon, as well as unidentified flying objects near the area designated the Sea of Tranquility. In July 1969, the Americans set out to make the first moon landing.

"T minus thirty seconds to takeoff," Commander Mitch Campbell heard through the comm system.

As he sat strapped in, he thought back on the three tenuous years of training he'd undergone to prepare for this mission. Next to him was his copilot, Lieutenant Cal Roberts. Surrounded by computer screens and gauges, he readied himself for the 400,000 pounds of thrust he would soon experience.

The blast was sudden. He was going nearly 200 miles per hour before the spacecraft had cleared the launch tower. The roar of the engines was deafening, and the spacecraft shook violently as it left Earth's atmosphere.

A few minutes later, Commander Campbell heard the rocket boosters disengage, and what had been a turbulent ride turned into a peaceful glide through the vastness of space. He looked out his cockpit window towards the blue planet they'd left behind. He was struck by how small the world looked from space, which in turn made him contemplate his even lesser importance in the universe.

"Jesus Christ, Mitch, that was one hell of a ride!" Roberts screamed through the intercom.

"It sure was."

They spent the next few days traveling towards the moon then moved to the lunar module *Eagle* to begin their descent. When they arrived, the commander was shocked by what he saw out his side cockpit window.

"What the fuck are those? Lieutenant, switch to a secure line and radio NASA immediately," Campbell ordered.

In the distance were three bright lights that appeared to be escorting them as they descended. The two astronauts both sat in an eerie silence. They continued with their mission as they had been trained to do, but what they saw next chilled them to the bone.

"NASA mission control. *Eagle*, go ahead."

"We're not alone up here," was all Campbell could muster.

"What do you see?" Mission Control asked.

"Well, umm, for lack of a better explanation, I'm seeing something that looks like Ancient Egypt crossed with a modern city. There are pyramids, buildings, and a fleet of spaceships that are fucking huge," Campbell responded.

"Do not, I repeat *do not* live-stream your exit from the module," Mission Control commanded. "We'll play the prerecorded version."

Before Campbell could reply, the module lost all communication with Mission Control. The visual radar had been jammed, and neither he nor Lieutenant Roberts had control of the spacecraft.

"I don't know who's flying this thing, but it sure as hell isn't us!" Roberts cried.

Frantically, Campbell unstrapped himself and made his way to the emergency storage locker, where he pulled out two fully automatic rifles.

"I don't know if these will do us any good, but here," he said, handing Roberts one of the rifles.

Once the *Eagle* had flawlessly landed, Campbell and Roberts stared in awe at what they could see outside. Vehicles approached them at speed. They looked like Earth vans yet they had no wheels—they hovered two feet off the ground with no detectable propulsion system.

What they witnessed next left them questioning the very fabric of reality.

Out of the first vehicle stepped seven black men and women nearly eight foot tall. They carried no weapons and were dressed in what Campbell would have described as a modern-day Egyptian spacesuit. They wore no helmets, and seemed to have no need for oxygen.

Two of the giants immediately opened the back door of the second vehicle, and a black woman stepped out. She was dressed similarly to the others, but her uniform was distinctly different—it had the flair of an Egyptian goddess. She was clearly the leader. She stood facing the *Eagle*, flanked by what appeared to be her subordinates.

Campbell and Roberts were completely taken aback. To finally have confirmation of alien life was a lot to take in, but the fact that they were black went against everything society had taught them.

Quickly pulling himself together, Campbell looked at Roberts and, in a deceptively calm voice, said, "Well, Lieutenant, I suppose it's time to meet our hosts."

Lieutenant Roberts didn't reply. The very thought of black aliens had left him speechless—everything he had known and thought had just come crashing down on him.

They exited the *Eagle* and approached the human-like entities with their weapons raised.

"Those are not needed and quite useless," the black lady said.

As soon as she uttered those words, both astronauts stood stunned as their grip on the rifles involuntarily released. Their weapons levitated and gently landed on the steps of the *Eagle*.

"Such a terrible way to greet your creators. However, we understand your barbaric ways—therefore, we are not offended. I am Sekhmet, Ruler of the Desert. I have been instructed to receive you—your mother wishes to speak with you before you depart this heavenly post."

When Campbell entered the transport vehicle, he was amazed to see a small computer-like flat screen. The pilot of the craft would touch certain areas of the screen and vocally issue directions, as if the screen itself was piloting the craft. He sat shellshocked and confused.

What the hell is going on? Mother... heavenly post... What the fuck is going on here? Campbell wondered.

Less than two minutes later, they arrived at their destination—a huge building that resembled the many temples and palaces in Ancient Egypt. There was a large sphinx on each side of the entrance, and the building, like the sphinxes, was made of gold. Both Campbell and Roberts were escorted inside, where Nephthys and her royal guard awaited them.

Jesus Christ, is outer space run by fucking women? Lieutenant Roberts thought.

"Lieutenant Roberts, it is not a matter of running anything. You would be best to view it as guidance. Allow me to introduce myself, for I am Nephthys, mistress of the house," Nephthys said matter-of-factly.

He was stunned that Nephthys had just heard his thoughts.

"We can communicate verbally or telepathically," she told him. "The choice is entirely up to you. Follow me, for there is one who wishes to speak with you."

Nephthys led them down a long hall lined on both sides with what appeared to be soldiers. They approached a golden platform that floated two inches off the floor. Nephthys stepped upon the platform and directed the astronauts to do the same.

"Have no fear," she said before the platform lifted them to the twelfth floor in the blink of an eye.

Nephthys quickly ushered them through two double doors that resembled a temple entrance. Inside, sitting behind a large desk, was Lilith. Satan stood behind her.

The astronauts trembled before them with awe and fear.

"Have no fear," Satan said, smiling as he made his way over to the astronauts.

"Who are you?" Campbell asked, apprehension evident in his voice.

"I am your adversary, who was against your creation, but I'm nonetheless your salvation," Satan replied as he walked out of the office.

Against my creation? Who the fuck are these beings? Campbell wondered.

Lilith rose from the desk and walked over to Campbell and Roberts. "It is a shame that you don't recognize your mother. For it was I, Lilith, who created humans. Your arrogance, along with your fear, has you confused right now. We have been with you from the beginning, and I am somewhat of a pleased mother, yet very disturbed by the actions of humans. You have made great technological progress, but your overall mentality remains warlike and abusive.

"You have mistreated the ancestors of my brothers and sisters, though their only intention was to free you. You have made it to space, but your motivation was earthly domination. There were many that wanted your annihilation and even attempted this with a great flood. It was my husband that saved you—the same being you demonized.

"Those whose appearance differs from yours have been demoted from princes and queens to servants and whores, for on Earth servants are upon horses, while princes walk as servants. You have noticed that here women are set in great dignity, but on Earth you view the woman as your property, inferior to man. Have you not considered that it is a woman you have sprouted from?

"It is for these reasons that you are never to return here again. It is wise that you heed my words, for one shall honor their mother and father if their days will be long on the Earth. Go back and tell the humans what you have seen here. Relay my words to them, and correct these errors of thoughts and actions. Your time is short, for I am the fourth. You will not know your appointed time. Like a thief in the night, I shall return riding a white horse. And every knee shall bow, and every tongue shall confess."

SATAN

The moment I walked into the halls of the Eternal Tribunal, I knew that Jehovah's plan had many flaws. The very thought that life could be created with expectations of stagnation was foolish. To further compound the problem, the beauty of the Earth women made it impossible that the seeds of gods would never be sowed within them.

Before time was not, the gods existed, and harmonious balance reigned supreme throughout the universe. How the concept of servitude was deemed necessary by the Eternal Tribunal, I am to this day unsure, for the idea of slavery goes against the grain of love.

My brother Jehovah has always struggled with pride. He has indeed despised the power of the goddess—as a child, he was reprimanded many times for trying to rule over the female energy force.

From the beginning, I had no thoughts to rebel, nor could I have imaged that I would lie with Eve. I must confess that Eve's death brought great grief. Such a sorrow I have never known. However, when I told Eve that she would surely not die, I did not lie to her. Finality does not exist. There is no end, only change, and after Eve enjoyed a brief period in the chambers of rest, I once again reunited with her when she took the form of Keziah, the daughter of Job.

There has always been one constant throughout my existence of no beginnings. I am speaking of my beloved wife

Lilith, for there is none that I love more than her. She has been instrumental in all I have done. Her wisdom is a flaming torch which has always guided my way. Her creative womb bears witness to gods and manifests all subconscious thoughts that are ejaculated righteously within her.

The inhabitants of Earth would do well in ceasing to transform prophets into gods. Additionally, mortal man would benefit greatly by humbly accepting his origins. It is no mystery that man comes from the womb of a woman, yet the origin of the goddess shall forever be a mystery to those cloaked in mortal flesh.

I tell you without shame that I, Satan, am indeed mighty, but it is Lilith's female energy source, the divine conduit of the universe, that brings this to be. With faith in her foresight, I naturally accepted the framework she so cleverly devised. Many a man has failed to concede to what has been, what is, and what will forever be; however, with great love, compassion, and understanding for those found worthy, the goddess shall surely raise them from the grave of ignorance which mortals erroneously refer to as hell.

In a variety of ways, the goddess protects and nurtures her offspring. The legacy of Mary Magdalene and her most learned disciple John is an example of this, for it was I that gave my only begotten son for the salvation of the peoples of Earth. It was Lilith, however, that willingly suffered the indignity of man's scornful ways.

Such a humiliating sacrifice is beyond a mortal's level of comprehension. Most of the inhabitants of Earth have never been initiated into the black rites of the goddess, which is an unfortunate result of my brother's trickery.

Through religion, Jehovah replaced the mind of the universe with that of a servant. Woman's creative genius was deceptively hidden while mortal man was placed upon a throne of illusion—a throne in which nowhere throughout the Universe will one find the male energy source.

This act was, and is, the sole cause for the quarantine of Earth, for it wasn't the interbreeding of gods and Earth women that put the universe in such an inharmonious state but Jehovah's act of negating the true creative source. This chaos has infiltrated the magnetic fields of Earth and has established so many absurd patterns of thought. The Earthlings are over-whelmed by abnormalities. They are not able to perceive the natural order of the universe. Truth has been distorted, and what was once known to be reality is now mistakenly viewed as fantasy.

My offspring have been rendered incapable of distinguishing between their adversary and their savior. I have understood since time was not that my brother is the embodiment of the lie. He is truly the great deceiver. However, I, Satan, cannot pass judgement on him.

I must confess, my children's inability to recognize their father pains me greatly. Instead, they have designated me as the source and instigator of all their calamities, even the effects they experience from their own causes.

Ages ago, my dear wife Lilith lit the torch illuminating the path, for she is the woman that shines brightly. Her light shines in the darkness, and the darkness has yet to understand it.

Wandering in the wilderness, they have grown to despise the light which was intended to lead the way; their evil thoughts have caused the light to blind them, which is what the universe mandates, for only those pure in thought can be guided by the goddess.

And so, it is with faith, hope, and charity that I continue to aid my children as any loving father would.

WISDOM OF THE THREE MARYS

Love is the balance between good and evil. Being nonrestrictive in nature, it knows no boundaries—it's an act of being and an act of doing, for none know where it comes, nor where it shall go.

Love is inherent in our very being. Therefore, to go in search of this awesome gift is futile. One must concede to this truth in order to cherish oneself—in so doing, one is prepared to share this gift.

For love to coexist in harmony, the elements must be complimentary to one another. Fire needs the air to fuel its flames, while the Earth needs water to cultivate its soil. Let these things fall into accordance with the receiving, stabilizing, and redirecting of energies.

It is wise to never confuse loving with possessing. This illusion only leads to the need to control the uncontrollable. Be wary of a society that condemns the outward affection of love, for none can label, classify, or regulate who or how one loves. There is no adequate definition of the word love because it simply is, as you are, and I am.

Sex is both a pleasure and a great responsibility. From this most intense pleasure sprouts the carrier for the soul. Therefore, when man procreates with woman, he has become as god. The ebb and flow of creation is *all*.

Once this is understood, sex reverts to an act of pure pleasure, and should be pursued and enjoyed as such. Restricting or restraining one's sexual desires is not conducive to one's happiness; taboos and so-called forbidden sex acts are a direct assault upon the sanctity of the woman.

The power of the woman resides between her legs. For this reason, she has been conditioned to sit with her legs crossed. Seductive clothing is frowned upon; her promiscuity is scorned, simply because the priests of men fear her. They know that if her true identity is exposed, their worthless, invisible god shall be also.

The promiscuous woman should be revered, for she is not delusional, nor easily misled. There shall be only one law regulating the matters of sex: if your desires feel good to act upon and harm none, then yield to them without shame. It would be sinful not to.

Jealousy, possessiveness, and selfish behavior should never be part of one's sexual experiences. True love would never restrict another in their sexual desires. True love would never hinder one from receiving pleasure from others, regardless of whether one is a friend, intimate partner, husband, or wife. The intimate practice of loving through sexual relations can exist on numerous levels. Selfish behavior and jealousy cannot.

LILITH

There have been many things said and written about me. I, like nature herself, have hidden my secrets for all to see. The masses remain oblivious to my wisdom, yet for the few, I have afforded a glimpse of the white light that I shine. Some have dared to lift the veil from my face only to discover another.

I am the mother of all that is, has been, and forever will be. My wisdom is sought after yet unattainable. My voice is numerous, yet I am unheard. My message is your saving grace, and for this reason my messengers are crucified daily.

Satan is not only my loving husband but brother as well. He is the strike of the match that produced our daughter. I, of course, am the result of such intercourse. How you perceive me will be nothing more than the effect of your cause. For some, my flame brings warmth and life, while others burn from their own impurities.

Throughout the universe, it is known that manifestation comes to be through the creative womb of the goddess; therefore, I assert that none should worship any other god but me. However, worship is not what I require, nor have a need for. A proper application of the dark rites of the goddess is deemed acceptable, for unconditional love is the only means of producing good fruit. Possession is but an illusion. Control is but a weakness. Disregarding the goddess is blasphemy and brings discontent. From the womb of a goddess, man came to be, but the origin of the goddess is enigmatic to the mortal mind.

I have sacrificed much for my children. My submission to Joseph was offensively pleasurable, an act that exiled me from Heaven for eternity. Just as I was with every Jesus, Muhammad, Buddha, Lao Tzu, and many other great prophets, I will be with you. I will never leave you or forsake you. My daughters will be with you always, to the end of the age.

All is one and one is all. The wise understand that all is love. Man's search for God is futile if he doesn't search within, and his arrival at the gates of inner peace shall never be without me at his side, for polarity exists in everything, and therefore, he must have his opposite to create the one.

The universe responds to such. Energy is the master, while servitude is the concession; when the will is aligned with the source, the mind produces a glorious conception.

Let all understand that there is always a coming and going. What is today shall not be tomorrow, for permanence is but an illusion and change is God. All is ebb and flow. Therefore, have no fear. There is nothing that is stationary. Everything is everything, and all is life. Everything vibrates. The physical vibrates slowly, while the soul vibrates rapidly. Control your frequency, and you will control your reality.

As it is in Heaven, so it shall be on Earth. As it is on Earth, so it shall be in Heaven. Once the two are merged, the sacred union shall be consummated.

There are no coincidences—everything happens according to the will of the Mother. All travel east on the wheel of destiny. All shall be subjected to the same twelve influential energies. Therefore, it is best to judge none.

The male and female energy source are one—there is nothing in this space-time continuum that does not observe this truth, for when separation exists, dissension is sure to follow.

For I am the light as well as the darkness. I build and I destroy. I bring peace and create chaos. I, Lilith, do all these things. My thoughts are not as your thoughts. My ways are incomprehensible. Out of my chaos springs order.

For I am the mystery, Babylon the Great, the mother of all harlots and abominations of the Earth. I am drunk with the blood of the saints. I am the one who was greatly admired. For I am the one with whom kings of the Earth have fornicated while drinking from my golden cup of misery, for my light blinds the selfish souls and leads the way for those with charitable hearts.

There are many universal laws, with love being the supreme law. To know me, you must be love. To walk with me, you must know thyself. To keep me by your side, your thoughts must be rooted in love.

I, Lilith, am the alpha and omega. All has begun with me. I am the truth and the way. For verily I say unto you that none shall see the Mother but through me. So it shall be!

The Inception